FOUR SEASONS OF MYSTERY

A COLLECTION OF GRAY WHALE INN STORIES

KAREN MACINERNEY

GRAY WHALE PRESS

Copyright © 2020 by Karen MacInerney

All rights reserved.

No part of this book may be reproduced in any form or by any electronic or mechanical means, including information storage and retrieval systems, without written permission from the author, except for the use of brief quotations in a book review.

This book is a work of fiction. Names, characters, places, and incidents are either products of the author's imagination or used fictitiously. Any resemblance to actual events or locales or persons, living or dead, is entirely coincidental.

Other books in the Gray Whale Inn Mysteries:

The Gray Whale Inn Mysteries

Murder on the Rocks

Dead and Berried

Murder Most Maine

Berried to the Hilt

Brush With Death

Death Runs Adrift

Whale of a Crime

Claws for Alarm

Scone Cold Dead

Anchored Inn

Cookbook: The Gray Whale Inn Kitchen

Blueberry Blues (A Gray Whale Inn Short Story)

Pumpkin Pied (A Gray Whale Inn Short Story)

Iced Inn (A Gray Whale Inn Short Story)

INTRODUCTION

Welcome to the first collection of Gray Whale Inn stories! There's one for each season, along with a bonus short story, Altar Flowers, which first appeared in *Portland Monthly* many years ago and has never before been published in book form.

I hope you enjoy reading these stories as much as I enjoyed writing them. And if you finish these hungry for more, stay tuned for a new series set in Maine... the new Snug Harbor mysteries, featuring Max Sayers, fledgling proprietor of Seaside Cottage Books! (You'll have a chance to meet her in Anchored Inn, the tenth Gray Whale Inn mystery.)

The debut book of the series, A Killer Ending, will be out Summer 2020. I'll be including a sneak peek and a chance to pre-order your copy at the end of Anchored Inn!

INTRODUCTION

Thank you so much for your support. Without you, there would be no Gray Whale Inn. Natalie and I are grateful for you each and every day.

XXX OOO

Karen

BLUEBERRY BLUES

BLUEBERRY BLUES

It was the Saturday of the Cranberry Island clambake, and I was beginning to wonder whether offering up the Gray Whale Inn as a location for the annual event was one of my better ideas. It was usually held at the island's church— Saint James Episcopal— but since the church floor refinishing project that was supposed to be done two months ago still hadn't been completed, I'd volunteered the Gray Whale Inn as an alternate location.

"Can't we put them out on the back deck?" I asked my best friend Charlene as she lugged a tub of clams into the inn's kitchen. The two of us had laid out sheets of plastic so any condensation— or leaky tubs— wouldn't hurt the pine floors. Since moving from Texas to open the inn six months earlier, my budget had been tight enough; the last thing I needed was to have to refinish my own floors.

"Are you kidding me?" Charlene pursed her glossy lips and shook her head as we maneuvered another load through the kitchen door. For a storekeeper on a little island off the coast of Maine, she always managed to look fabulous. Forget flannel and fisherman's sweaters; today's ensemble was a green velour sweater and tight jeans, with a crystal necklace and earrings that sparkled in the morning light. The overall effect was dampened only slightly by the apron she'd borrowed to protect her outfit— it was white with big black spots, featuring two dancing cows and the logo "Moo-stepping in Texas."

As Charlene adjusted her grip on the clams, it occurred to me that she'd be an excellent subject for the *Daily Mail*. The new staff reporter, Andi Jordan, was heading over with a photographer to cover the clambake, and I was hoping for some good coverage for the inn. Since taking the job at the paper, she'd written harsh reviews for several local restaurants, but since it was an island-wide event, I crossed my fingers that she'd focus on the community focus of the event— and the beauty of the inn. My bookings calendar wasn't exactly overflowing, and I needed all the publicity I could get. Glancing down at my frayed sweatshirt, I reflected that it would probably be a good idea to slip into something more photogenic before everyone arrived.

"We can't put them on the deck," Charlene said as we bumped past the pine table. "The clams have to be inside. Otherwise the seagulls would gulp them all down in ten minutes flat." We deposited the tub of clams on the floor, and she reached up to adjust her hair. "Besides, this way they're closer to the stove. How many pots do you have, anyway?"

"I've got two big ones, plus the one you promised to bring over." I surveyed the crowded kitchen floor. "Although how we're going to manage to cook in here with all that stuff, I don't know."

"Don't worry about it," she said. "Emmeline's taking care of the corn."

"Yeah, but I still have twelve more blueberry pies to bake." I nodded toward the pies already lined up by the refrigerator, and the huge bags of rolls that covered half of my countertops. "At least I don't have to do the rolls."

"I just hope the tables and chairs get here soon." Charlene glanced out at the lawn behind the house— it was a brilliant emerald green, fading into a field of blue and pink lupines and the rocks and water below it. I'd sweet-talked my neighbor— and maybe-boyfriend— John into mowing it yesterday, and had spent a few hours weeding the flowerbeds as he worked, surreptitiously admiring the long brown legs extending from his faded cut-offs. The smell of the beach roses, sweet peas and fresh-cut grass, mixed with the ever-present salt tang of the sea, was a tonic; if I could bottle it, I'd make millions.

"Is that all?" I asked as we lugged the last tub in from Charlene's pick-up.

"Unless you want to help me track down the tables and chairs..." "I've got blueberry pies to make, remember? Besides," I said, nodding toward the overflowing sink, "I haven't finished cleaning up from breakfast."

∽

"WHEN DO we get to try one of your legendary pies?"

I replaced a tray of clams and turned to smile at Andi Jordan, the reporter from the *Daily Mail*. She was a young woman in her twenties, with blunt-cut hair and a pair of wire-rimmed glasses that reminded me of John Lennon's. The clambake was in full swing, and the clams were disappearing as fast as I could put them out.

"First we have to finish off the clams," I told Andi, who had a little bit of clam juice on her sharp chin. She was so thin I was longing to sit her down at my table and give her an entire pie. With an extra helping of ice cream. Next to her stood a lanky, good-looking young man with a camera.

My eyes lingered on the camera slung around his neck and the tripod tucked under his arm. I gave the inn a quick critical glance. The white-curtained windows sparkled in the afternoon light, and the window boxes overflowed with sweet peas, verbena, and brilliant fuchsia geraniums. A breeze from the sea brought a whiff of beach roses wafting over me, mixing with the delicious scents of fresh rolls and clams. Everything looked perfect. I hoped the photographer would snap several shots of the inn; I could use the press.

I turned back to Andi. "Well, since that was the last pot, I'd say we're just about ready to move on to dessert." I surveyed the crowd of islanders spread across the sloping green lawn. They were wolfing down the food faster than we could bring it out. "You'd think they hadn't eaten in weeks," I said. "I hope we've got enough."

"I've heard you specialize in pastries," Andi said. "I'm looking forward to trying the pie."

"You can have the first piece. I promise."

My friend Charlene spotted us by the table. She hustled over to see us, the cow apron still clinging to her ample curves. "Do you think it's time for pie?"

"That's just what Andi was asking," I said. "I think so."

As Andi and the photographer helped themselves to another few clams, Charlene and I headed back to the kitchen and started lugging out pies. "Too bad you didn't get Gertrude," she whispered.

"Gertrude Pickens? The reporter who just about accused me of murder a few months ago? No, thank you," I said.

"I don't trust this Andi woman," Charlene said. "Did you see what she wrote about that new bakery in Bar Harbor last week?"

"The one with those delicious apple turnovers?" I asked.

Charlene nodded. "Ms. Jordan evidently found them dry."

"Uh oh," I said, casting a glance at the reporter, who was lingering near the pie table while the photographer snapped shots of the spread. She definitely did not have the build of a woman dedicated to the sampling of baked goods. I glanced down at the pie in my hand. The crust had turned out perfectly— golden brown lattice over beds of dark, plump Maine blueberries. How could she find fault with it? I set a fresh pie on the table and cut a large piece— it was still a bit warm— for Andi, saying a small, silent prayer.

The islanders, smelling pie, swarmed the dessert table behind her as she examined the piece with a critical eye. "Did you bake all of these?"

"All twenty-four of them."

"They look just delicious. If they taste as good as they look, maybe we could put the recipe in the paper."

I beamed at her, my worries dispelled. "That would be great."

"My photographer has been shooting all morning, but do you mind if we get a few shots of you in front of the inn?"

Did she mind? I would have begged for it. I reached up to adjust the collar of the silk blouse I had donned with just such a contingency in mind. "That would be great."

"How about if we get a shot of you with one of the pies? I love the lattice tops. They're beautiful!"

"That would be great!" I said. "Let me just go and get a few more pies for the table." Charlene was slicing, but could barely keep up with the demand; the plates were already disappearing fast. "I'll be right back."

"Irving!" Andi hollered at her photographer, who had wandered off somewhere, as I hurried back to the kitchen for more pies. I paused to smooth my hair down and add a bit of lipgloss, then headed back outside, pie in hand, to an empty table in the corner of the yard where Irving was assembling his tripod.

"I thought we'd get the inn in the background of the shot," he said.

My kind of guy, I thought. Maybe I'd give him a whole pie, just for himself.

I stood smiling, the pie held in front of me, the inn behind me, as Irving fiddled with the camera. Just as he snapped the first shot, a flurry of activity broke out at the edge of the lawn. I looked over just in time to see Henry Hoyle bending over and clutching his stomach.

Andi, who had been asking me questions about the inn and jotting down my answers, paused with her pen mid-stroke. Her sharp eyes focused on Henry's plaid-covered back.

"What's wrong with him, I wonder?" I asked.

"I don't know," she said, "but he's not the only one." As we watched, two more people staggered up from their chairs and doubled over, clutching their stomachs.

"I'll be right back," Andi said, pushing her chair back and calling Irving to join her. She hurried over to where Henry was wiping his forehead. "Looks like we got a case of food poisoning!" she yelled as she trotted over to where now three more people had started groaning. I winced as the murmur of concern instantly escalated to a roar.

"Somebody call the doctor!" yelled a squat man I didn't recognize. I turned and ran into the inn—partly to call the doctor and partly so I wouldn't have to watch the fiasco unfolding in my back yard.

～

BY THE TIME I had gotten in touch with the Bar Harbor Hospital and asked them to send over medical assistance, almost half a dozen people were suffering from stomach cramps. As I filled glasses with ice water to take to the afflicted, Charlene burst into the kitchen.

"It's a nightmare out there," she said. "What do you think happened?"

"Gertrude said something about food poisoning," I said, "but I'm hoping it's just a stomach bug."

"Some stomach bug," she said. "On the plus side, at least the *Daily Mail* get a good story out of it."

I grimaced. "I can see the headline now: *Fifty people transported to hospital after lunch at Gray Whale Inn.*"

"I told you that reporter would be trouble." Charlene brushed a few crumbs off of her sweater. "Do you think it could it be the clams? We kept them on ice the whole time, though."

I sighed, looking out at the melee in the back yard. "I wish I knew."

"Sometimes I think maybe someone put the evil eye on you."

"Well if they did, the curse only seems to go active when someone from the press appears."

Charlene peeked into the cookie jar, withdrew an oatmeal cookie and said brightly, "See? It could be worse."

"How?"

"It's only a part-time curse."

∼

THE ARTICLE in the *Daily Mail* was every bit as bad as I had feared. *Fifteen Hospitalized after Dinner at Gray Whale Inn*, blared the headlines. *Police Suspect Food Poisoning.* Next to it were two photos: one of yours truly, proudly displaying a pie with the inn as a backdrop, and one of Gerald Whitestone with a plate of half-eaten pie in his hand and flanked by a policewoman and an EMT.

I crumpled the paper and tucked it into a drawer to read later, hoping that none of my guests would pick up today's issue down at the store. My plan to host the clambake had backfired. Instead of the residents of Cranberry Island going home full of clams, pie, and goodwill— and the island coffers overflowing with extra revenue— the day had ended with a phone call to Emergency Services. And an article about the inn that wasn't exactly scrapbook material.

When Charlene dropped off my copy of the *Daily Mail*, she said the paper was already sold out, bought up by the locals. Apparently the Clambake Catastrophe was the biggest news on the island in months. The only bright spot I could see was that I likely wouldn't be asked to host it again next year. It wasn't much.

According to the article, everyone except for Gerald Whitestone, who was 86 and severely dehydrated, had recovered and been sent home. The police had spent a lot of time poking around. And Andi Jordan, who of course had written the article, had included a nice shot of the uniformed officers on the front page, with the inn as a backdrop. Not exactly the kind of coverage I'd been hoping for. The police had taken samples of all the food served for testing. In fact, they were about to close my kitchen down until my neighbor and quasi-boyfriend John used his pull as island deputy to argue my case.

Thanks to his efforts, my kitchen was still open—for now.

Which was a good thing, because I had six guests coming down for breakfast in thirty minutes. Hopefully they weren't big newspaper readers. I banished thoughts of bad press and sick islanders from my mind and focused on the lemon-blueberry ricotta muffins I was baking for breakfast. The show, as they say, must go on.

I squeezed the last of the lemons and flipped open the trash can lid. A wad of legal paper that had been jammed into the trash tumbled onto the floor. I should have emptied the can before lugging it back, I thought to myself. But with all the hullabaloo, it had been overlooked. When I reached down to grab the papers, a brown plastic bottle clattered to the floor.

Why would someone wrap an empty bottle in yellow legal paper? I grabbed a paper towel and picked it up. It looked like a medicine bottle— but I knew I hadn't been the one to throw it into the trash. I opened it and sniffed, then replaced the lid quickly. Whatever it was, it sure wasn't vanilla extract.

~

"So what do you think happened?" Charlene asked as I stirred milk into my coffee down at the Cranberry Island Store. Once the guests had left and I'd cleaned the rooms, I'd decided to head down to visit my best friend— and see if she'd heard anything on the island grapevine. Besides, the big squishy couches and the smell of coffee and dried goods always made me feel cozy.

As I sipped my coffee, my friend reached up to pat her caramel-colored hair into place, then brushed an imaginary crumb off her black wraparound sweater. We might be in Maine, but Charlene wouldn't be caught dead in plaid flannel.

"I'm guessing the food was sabotaged," I said.

"What other explanation is there?" she said. "You cook all the time, and nothing like this has ever happened before."

"I wish I knew," I said. I told Charlene about the bottle I had dropped off with my neighbor John after breakfast. "He's going to take it over to the police lab on the mainland today. Maybe they'll be able to turn something up."

"You'd better hope there are fingerprints, too— and not just yours. Since you found it in your kitchen and all."

"Thanks for reminding me," I said.

Charlene peeled the wrapper from one of the Double-Berry Lemon Muffins I'd brought down and sank her teeth into it. "You know, I think this is one of my favorite recipes," she said.

"Mine too," I said, unwrapping my own muffin and anticipating the bright flavor of moist, lemon-scented cake studded with blueberries and raspberries. "I had a few leftover berries, so I decided to use them."

"They're terrific," Charlene said through a mouthful of muffin. "I keep thinking about yesterday, though. I wonder who might have done something like that? I mean, unless the clams were tainted, obviously someone tampered with the food — besides, doesn't food poisoning usually take a while to kick in?"

"More than fifteen minutes, I'd think."

"Exactly. I don't think it was the clams. Besides, since the only people who got sick were the ones who ate pie, I'm guessing that's the source."

I sighed and bit into a muffin. The bright lemony flavor wasn't enough to stave off the sinking feeling that had been haunting me all morning. I had stayed up half the night baking those pies— and as it turned out, they all had to be thrown away. Except for the ones the lab took for testing, of course. A copy of today's *Daily Mail* sat on the edge of the counter. I'd gotten publicity all right. Just not the kind I wanted.

But why?" I asked. "Why on earth would you want to poison half the island at a clambake?"

"Well, I heard Mabel was a bit sore that she wasn't in charge this year."

"Mabel Penney?"

Charlene nodded. "She's run it for the last several years, and got her nose out of joint when they told her you were going to be handling it."

"I had no idea," I said. "Still, is that really a motive for poisoning pies?"

"You never know," she said. "On the plus side, at least Andi got the front cover out of it. That means Gertrude might be on the way out."

"Andi is going to replace Gertrude Pickens?"

"They've been threatening to demote her to the obituary pages," Charlene said. "Making room for fresh blood, so to speak."

"I thought Gertrude was their crack reporter?"

Charlene finished off her muffin and dabbed at her lips with a napkin. "Not anymore," she said. "Apparently Andi's been moving up in the ranks."

"At least she hasn't said I was responsible for murder," I said. Gertrude had written a series of stories insinuating that I had murdered one of my guests recently, and I wasn't sure she'd gotten over the disappointment of being wrong.

Charlene glanced at the front page of the paper,

which featured a blown-up image of the inn, complete with several policemen. "Only food poisoning. At least so far."

"Not comforting," I said. Not at all.

~

A HALF HOUR LATER, I stepped out of the store into a beautiful early summer afternoon. A cool breeze riffled my hair, smelling of the roses that lined the front of the shop and tinged with the briny scent of the sea.

As climbed onto my Schwinn, I reflected that it was a good thing I rode my bike so darned much. Weight gain is an occupational hazard of innkeeping; with all of those delicious goodies at arm's reach, how could it not be?

I debated going back to the inn, but decided instead to point the bike toward Mabel Penney's house. Not that I was expecting her to admit poisoning my blueberry pies. In fact, I'm not sure what I was planning to do. But it was better than doing nothing— and besides, after eating three muffins, I could use the exercise.

Mabel's house was one of the pretty shingle-style houses that dotted the water's edge on the south side of the island, and my legs were feeling the burn by the time I pulled up to the driveway. I knew she rented it out for a few weeks in the summer and went to stay with her sister, and I could imagine she made a nice bit of extra money doing so. A screened porch wrapped around the little house, and the lupine-studded meadow below it sloped down to a rocky beach.

I parked my bike and walked down the path to the white-painted front door. Two pots filled with bright red geraniums flanked it, and wind chimes tinkled in the breeze. All in all, the little gray house looked like the on-site location for an L.L. Bean photo shoot.

I knocked at the door and tried to figure out what I was going to say. I didn't have long; a moment later the door opened, and Mabel's wizened face peered around it.

"Can I help you?" she said, sounding less than friendly.

"Hi," I said. "I'm sorry to drop in like this, but I was wondering if we could talk for a little bit?"

She pressed her thin lips together, then opened the door wider to admit me. "I suppose. I've only got a few minutes, though."

I followed her into the house, which smelled of lavender and the ever-present tang of the sea. The white curtains billowed in the breeze as she led me to her parlor, a cozy room filled with slipcovered couches and a beautiful blue rag rug. A pitcher of lupines, blazing purple and blue, decorated the coffee table, and little dishes of dried lavender dotted the hutch and end tables.

"Your house is beautiful," I said. And it was.

"Thank you," she said, thawing only slightly as we sat down on the pale blue couches. She retreated to the corner of one and crossed her arms.

I clasped my hands and leaned forward. "I was just talking with Charlene a few minutes ago, and I want to apologize."

Mabel's narrow eyebrows shot up. "Apologize?"

"When they asked me to take over the clambake, I didn't realize you had done it for so many years." She bit her lips.

"Well, you're the *professional*, I suppose."

"Still. You've done it for years, and from everything I've heard, it went off splendidly." I chuckled. "Hand it over to the professional, and half the island gets carted off to the hospital."

A smile tugged at the edge of her lips. "Bad luck, I guess."

"Do you think so?" I asked.

"What else would it be?" she said primly.

I looked at her hard. "Some people think someone tampered with the pies."

Her blue eyes didn't waver, and she shrugged. "I can't think why they would."

"Me neither," I said, studying her. "But since it turned out so disastrously.... I wonder if you'd be willing to take it back over next year?"

She shook her head sharply. "I don't think so. It's a lot of work, you see, and I'm not as young as I used to be. To be honest, it was a bit of relief."

Was it, I wondered? "Are you sure?"

Mabel nodded. "I think I'm done with the clambake." She glanced at her watch. "I hate to hurry you off, but I must be going. I have tea with a friend shortly, and I hate to be late."

"Can I use your restroom before I go?"

She sighed. "I suppose so. It's down the hall."

"Thanks."

The bathroom was as sweet as the rest of the house, decorated in white and lemon yellow. Once the door was shut behind me, I suppressed a twinge of conscience and opened the medicine cabinet, glancing through the contents.

Heart medication, wart remover, something that looked like it might be for diabetes. I was about to give up when a brown bottle caught my eye.

I pulled it down and read the yellowing label: Ipecac. The bottle was full; I unscrewed the lid and took a whiff, wrinkling my nose at the smell.

It was the same stuff I'd found in my trashcan that morning.

～

"Ipecac," I announced to Charlene at the store that afternoon.

My friend handed me a mug of coffee, pulled up a stool across the counter from me, and unsnapped the lid of the Tupperware I'd brought with me. "How do you know?"

"I found it in her medicine cabinet; it's the exact same bottle I found in the trash."

"Do you think she did it?" Charlene asked, helping herself to one of the brownies inside. "Just to get the clambake back to herself?"

"If so, she's changed her mind. I offered to let her host it again, and you'd have thought I wanted to send my overflow guests to her spare bedroom."

"So it's not Mabel. Who else might have it in for you?"

"There's a bakery over on the mainland that wanted the business," I said.

"The one that keeps trying to get me to sell their gluten-free muffins?" Charlene made a face. "They taste like baked cardboard."

"Still. The owner was here that day."

"Truc," she said. "Anyone else have it in for you?"

"Other than Andi Jordan?" I asked.

"Her photographer was pretty cute."

"He took a beautiful photo," I said, reaching for the *Daily Mail* at the end of the counter. The inn looked gorgeous, framed against the pine trees and the green grass. If only it weren't for the policemen — and Gerald Whitestone, hunched over and looking sickly, a plate of my half-eaten pie in his hand.

"Except for the sick guy eating your food," Charlene said helpfully.

"Why does this always happen to me?" I asked, pushing the paper away. "I can't look at it anymore."

"Bad luck," she said. Then, "Wait. What's that?"

"What?" I asked.

"There's somebody by the trash can. There, in the right-hand corner. Isn't that where you found the ipecac?"

I squinted at the photo. I couldn't make out who it was, but there was definitely a familiar-looking bottle in the person's hand.

"Did you get the photographer's number?" I asked Charlene.

"No," she said, licking a bit of chocolate off of a polished fingernail, "but I wish I had."

"Would you mind calling Gertrude and asking for it?"

"A bit forward, don't you think?" she asked, cocking an eyebrow.

"When has that stopped you before?"

She pursed her lips. "Good point," she said, and reached for the phone.

∽

WE ARRIVED at Bar Harbor Photography Studio late the next morning, after stopping for apple turnovers at the much maligned Corner Bakery. Charlene had dressed up for the occasion in a chiffon-like blouse with a brilliant green sweater that made her highlighted hair glow.

"Do you think he's single?" she asked as we stopped outside the small shop. Framed in the window were a number of landscape photographs, along with a few 'arty' shots in black and white. I preferred the landscapes to the images of rusty nails and broken-down doors, but to each her own.

"I didn't see a ring," I said. "Then again, I didn't look, either."

A bell jingled as we pushed through the door. The front room's white walls were covered in framed photographs, and a computer sat on an old wood desk in the corner. Irving appeared in a doorway that must have led to his studio in the back of the shop.

"Charlene, right?" he asked, smiling appreciatively at my friend. "And Natalie," he said, turning to me. "The innkeeper."

"Thanks so much for letting us come and see the photos," I said.

"I'm real sorry about what happened," he said. "I was hoping it would be a good publicity piece for you. I did get some nice shots of the inn. If you'd like them, I can let you have them at a discount— considering the circumstances."

"That would be great," I said.

"Why don't you pull up a chair and take a look?" he asked, gesturing toward the computer. "I pulled up the album for you. You can just click through and write down the names of any photos you're interested in."

"Thanks," I said, pulling up a chair in front of the computer.

"I'll be in the back if you need me," he said, and Charlene watched longingly as he disappeared again.

"No ring," she whispered, but I was already scanning the photos.

They started out innocently enough, with islanders smiling in front of heaps of clams. I fast-forwarded to the photo of Gerald, hoping we could zero in on the person with the bottle in her hand.

"This is the photo," I said, tracking down the shot. We zoomed in, but neither of us could identify the person holding the bottle; his or her face was lost in the shadow of a tree.

"Check the ones right before and right after," Charlene suggested. I did, but there was no sign of the mystery person— or the bottle. I leaned back in my chair, defeated.

"What now?" I asked.

Charlene peered at the screen. "Look— he did a whole series of the pie table." I clicked on one of the shots; it showed Charlene in her cow apron, a pie in each hand. "My God," she said. "I had no idea I looked so enormous in that apron!"

"It's a bad angle," I said, flipping through the photos quickly, looking for something— anything— that might shed light on what had happened that day. I was almost to the end of the series when Charlene grabbed my shoulder.

"Stop," she said, pointing to the screen. I looked, and did a double-take. There, in the corner of the table, was the person with the bottle. Only in this shot, there was no shadow obscuring the face, and the bottle in plain view— right over one of the pies.

"I can't believe it," she said, letting out a long, low

whistle.

~

"CAN I HELP YOU?" Andi Jordan eyed me coolly over her wire-rimmed glasses. Her office was on the second floor of the *Daily Mail* building, an old shingled house right near the center of Bar Harbor with a view of the village green. A sun catcher glinted in the window, and there was a photo of a chunky golden retriever on her desk.

"I've got some new information you might want to include in your next article about the clambake," I said.

"Oh? Did they find out what the problem was?" she asked, leaning back in her chair. "Was it the clams?"

"Ipecac," I said.

She blinked. "You put ipecac in the clams?"

"No," she said. "I didn't put ipecac in anything. And it wasn't in the clams. It was in the pie."

Andi was quiet for a moment. "Did some sort of toxicology report come back?" she asked.

"Not exactly," I said. "But I thought you might be interested in this." I laid the photo Irving had printed for us on her desk.

She leaned forward to study the photo, and the

color leached from her face. "Where did you get this?"

"Your photographer took the photo," I said.

"You have no right to it. I paid for the shoot. These photos belong to me."

"You set me up," I said. "You put ipecac in the pie so you could get a big story out of it."

"No," she said, grabbing the photo and crumpling it into a ball.

"That's just a copy," I said. "I have the original right here." I held up a CD.

I thought I saw tears welling behind the glasses. "I can explain," she said, her voice husky.

"I'm listening." I sat down in one of her visitors' chairs; Charlene pulled up the other one.

"I didn't mean to cause any harm," she said. "It's just... I need this job. It's the only one I could find, and with the newspaper industry doing what it's doing, there's talk of laying me off already."

"I heard the paper was increasing circulation." Charlene examined a flawless pink fingernail. "You were just hoping to move up the ranks, is my guess."

She said nothing.

"So you've been manufacturing stories," I said.

Andi swallowed.

"There weren't really rats in the kitchen at Eagle Lake Cafe, were there?" Charlene said.

The reporter looked down at her keyboard.

"Or cockroaches at the Moonshine Inn," I said.

"You can't tell my editor," she said, almost moaning. "I'll lose my job!"

"Too late," I said. "I'm sorry. They're printing a retraction tomorrow."

~

"WELL, all's well, that ends well," Charlene said as she popped a chocolate chip cookie into her mouth. She'd brought over the paper as soon as it hit the store; I'd thanked her by baking a batch of her favorite cookies— chocolate chip with dried cranberries and walnuts mixed in. "And don't they say that all press is good press?" she said through a mouthful of crumbs.

"This last article certainly is," I said, holding up the latest copy of the *Daily Mail*. *Innkeeper Exonerated: Local Reporter Suspected Of Poisoning Pies*.

"Think Andi will keep her job?" Charlene asked.

"I doubt it," I said.

"She seemed nice enough. Just... desperate."

"Nice people don't try to ruin local businesses just to make themselves look good," I said. "Still, I do feel sorry for her. She's young. I hope she's learned something."

"At least Gerald is out of the hospital."

"I'm glad to hear it," I said.

"And I've got more good news," Charlene said, looking impish.

"Uh oh," I said. "What? You have a date with the photographer?"

"Yes," she said. "We're going to dinner Friday night. But that's not what I was talking about."

I shook my head, marveling at my friend's ability to attract men. "What is it, then?"

"I hope you had fun baking all those pies this year."

"Oh, no," I said, sinking down into my chair. "No."

"Yes," she said, her impish look breaking into an evil grin. "You guessed it, Nat. They think you did such a terrific job that they've decided you should host it every year!"

I stifled a groan at the thought of rolling out the dough for all those lattice-topped pies. And the memory of half the island regurgitating them on my lawn. "Fine," I said, "if nobody else will step up to the plate."

"I knew you'd say yes," Charlene said. "You always do."

"It's my Achilles heel," I said. "But next year? I'm making cobbler."

DOUBLE-BERRY LEMON MUFFINS

INGREDIENTS

- 1/2 cup lemon yogurt
- 3 tablespoons vegetable oil
- 1 tablespoon lemon juice
- 1 egg
- 1/2 teaspoon lemon extract (optional)
- 1 1/2 cups all-purpose flour
- 3/4 cup white sugar
- 2 teaspoons baking powder
- 1/4 teaspoon salt
- 1 teaspoon grated lemon zest
- 1/2 cup raspberries
- 1/2 cup blueberries
- 2 tablespoons coarse sugar

DIRECTIONS

1. Preheat the oven to 400 degrees. Grease or line 12-muffin pan with muffin cups.
2. In a large bowl, mix together the lemon yogurt, oil, lemon juice, eggs, and lemon extract.
3. In a separate bowl, stir together the flour, 3/4 cup sugar, baking powder, salt, and lemon zest.
4. Add the wet ingredients to the dry, and mix until just blended (lumps are good). Gently stir in the berries.
5. Spoon batter evenly into the prepared muffin cups and sprinkle coarse sugar over the tops.
6. Bake for 15 to 17 minutes in the preheated oven, or until the top springs back when lightly touched. Cool muffins in the pan on a wire rack.

PUMPKIN PIED

PUMPKIN PIED

"Have you heard about the new ghost?"

Charlene Kean sat at my big pine farm table, sipping a cup of the spiced coffee I'd made for us as I stirred a bit of lemon zest into a bowl of pumpkin pie filling. She'd taken the afternoon off from her duties as Cranberry Island's postmistress and storekeeper and was keeping me company as I worked on a new recipe for Turtle Pumpkin Pie, which I was hoping to enter into the pie contest at the upcoming Harvest Festival. The warm yellow kitchen of the Gray Whale Inn was filled with the autumnal scents of nutmeg and cloves, and the maple tree outside my kitchen window blazed red in the afternoon light. It was another magical October day at the Gray Whale Inn.

"What ghost?" My college roommate Lucy, who was visiting from Texas, walked into the kitchen as I gave the filling a last stir and poured it into the pie shell, I'd made earlier. She hung up her jacket on the peg and sat down next to Charlene. Her long brown hair was pulled up into a ponytail; despite a few strands of silver, she hardly looked older than she did when we were at school together.

"Hey, Lucy. How was your walk?" I asked. "Marvelous," she said. She smiled; her eyes bright.

"It's so good to be out of Houston, where it's still 1,000 degrees." She turned to Charlene. "I want to hear about the ghost!"

"I'm waiting to hear, too." I knew there was a resident ghost at the inn, although I hadn't encountered her for years, and there had been rumors of a ghost ship just offshore, but I hadn't heard about this one. "You don't think somebody's just been reading too many scary stories? It's almost Halloween."

"Even Eleazer told me he saw it," Charlene said, her mascaraed eyes wide. "By the field where the harvest festival is."

"Eli? That's not a big surprise. He believes in ghosts," I said.

"He's got good reason to," Charlene said. "He's seen a few in his day."

I had too, come to think of it—or at least had experiences I couldn't explain any other way.

Goosebumps rose on my arms as I thought of some of the things I'd seen since moving to the island. I slid the pie into the oven and set the timer, then reached for a bag of pecans. "Where is this new ghost hanging out?"

"It's right near the harvest festival, actually—in the woods by the corn maze," Charlene said, sipping her coffee. "There's a rumor that there's an old Indian burial ground there."

"I heard something about that. Didn't someone find a shell midden near it awhile back?" I asked as I measured out pecans.

Charlene nodded. "One of the archeology professors at Bowdoin was talking about opening up a dig site, but they never got around to it. And now that Eileen Franklin has passed and the property is up for sale, it'll probably never happen."

"It's sad, isn't it?" I asked. The town harvest festival had been held in the meadow for as long as anyone could remember; it belonged to Eileen, and she had donated use of it to the islanders. She'd passed a few months ago, though, and her off-island children were selling the property to a wealthy family from Boston.

"Maybe you can get some kind of archeological exemption," Lucy said, looking thoughtful. "I mean, if it's a burial ground… aren't there limits to what you can build?"

"Just because there's a midden nearby doesn't mean it was a graveyard," I pointed out as I added a hunk of butter and the pecans to a bowl, my mouth already watering at the thought of the praline topping.

"Maybe, but lots of people are reporting seeing weird lights down there at night," Charlene said, reaching up to unstick her eyelashes. Unlike the rest of us islanders, Charlene was always perfectly turned out, much to the admiration of the local lobstermen. Today she wore a red cashmere sweater with a pair of dark-washed jeans that clung to her ample but curvy figure. "Not just Eli. It's been all the talk down at the store." As postmistress of Cranberry Island and the owner of the general store, Charlene heard just about everything that happened on the island.

"Probably flashlights," I said, reaching for the brown sugar.

"Not from what I've heard. People who've seen it say it's kind of flickery and comes out late at night. And you know that garden Henry put in down there?"

"Yeah," I said, adding the brown sugar to the saucepan and turning the burner on low. I'd heard all about Henry's garden—as had the rest of the island. He'd planted pumpkins in May, feeding them weekly with his family's secret tea and maple syrup recipe, and couldn't stop talking about the orange monsters he'd been growing. Everyone else had harvested their pumpkins before the first frost, but he'd erected a greenhouse and, I'd heard, a portable heater to keep them warm. As a result, he was a shoo-in for the Cranberry Island Harvest Festival's big pumpkin contest—or at least that's what he'd been telling everyone who would listen for the past several weeks.

"Well, there seems to be a blight on his pumpkin patch. People are saying it's because it's on cursed land."

"More likely to be squash bugs," I suggested.

"Well, I think we should go check it out."

I stopped stirring. "Check out the pumpkin patch?"

"No, silly. The ghost." When I didn't respond, she leaned forward in her chair. "It'd be fun. I'll bring a batch of my pumpkin whoopie pies, you can bring a thermos of cider… we'll sit on a blanket under the stars."

"Can't we do that on my back porch?"

"But then we wouldn't see the ghost!" Charlene pointed out.

"But… what about everything here?"

"You don't have any paying guests, John's in Ellsworth with his mother, and Gwen's in California. So, unless you think Biscuit will die of loneliness, I think you're safe."

I followed her eyes to my orange tabby, who was asleep in her usual spot on the radiator. She didn't even flick an ear at the mention of her name.

I sighed. "Okay. But there'd better be whoopie pie."

"There will be," she said, finishing off her coffee and standing up. "I'm headed over to make them right now. I'll pick you up at 7; I'm counting on you for the hot spiced cider."

"I'll be the photographer," Lucy volunteered.

"Maybe mulled wine would be a better choice," I said as my friend bustled out the door toward her truck.

∼

The warm afternoon had faded to chilly twilight by the time we started trundling down a narrow forest path toward the meadow, laden with blankets, thermos, and a large Tupperware container filled with Charlene's famous whoopie pies. Charlene had insisted on parking well away from the site, so that no one would see us.

"I thought you said it was a ghost," I complained as I tripped over a tree root. (Charlene had forbidden flashlights, too.)

"I said it might be a ghost," she corrected me.

"And ghosts are offended by pick-up trucks and flashlights?"

"Shh," she reprimanded me. It was a good thing she'd brought whoopie pies, I thought as a branch whacked me in the face. "Sorry about that," Charlene whispered from somewhere in front of me.

"And I thought we Texans knew how to have fun," Lucy said.

"It's always a barrel of laughs with Charlene," I said, comfortable that I was far enough behind Charlene that she couldn't whack me.

It couldn't have been more than a quarter mile, but it felt like we'd been tramping through the woods for hours when Charlene decided we'd arrived at a likely spot.

"We can see it from here," she said. She was right; our location gave us a view not only of the corn maze and the stalls that had been put up for the harvest festival, but of the glowing tent-like structure about fifty yards away.

"That's the greenhouse?" Lucy asked.

"Everyone else has harvested their pumpkins, but he's keeping it warm through the frost. He's growing a monster, apparently."

"I thought we were here to see a ghost, not a giant pumpkin."

"We couldn't see it if we wanted to," she told Lucy and me as she shook out the blanket and laid it down on the grass. "He's got that thing wrapped up like it's the crown jewels."

I helped her straighten the blanket and sat down on it, reaching for the thermos. Hot cider sounded pretty darned good right now; my sneakered feet were chilled from the damp grass, and my light jacket wasn't enough to stave off the frost in the air. "How much is the contest worth?" I asked as I unscrewed the lid.

"A hundred dollars," she said. "But it's the bragging rights he's after. It's been hotly contested for years."

"I guess when you live on an island, you've got to make your entertainment," Lucy said with a grin as I filled mugs with cider. "Where are those whoopie pies?" she asked.

"Right here," Charlene said, and I heard the sound of a lid being removed. She handed each of us a moist cake sandwich cookie; I took a big bite.

"This almost makes it worth it," I mumbled through a mouthful of crumbs.

"I'll say," Lucy said. "Although I should have brought another sweatshirt."

"Just you wait," Charlene told me. "I have a feeling about tonight."

"So do I," I replied. "A cold and damp one." I took another swig of cider, and we settled in to wait.

We'd been sitting for about an hour when I started to think about going home. My foot kept falling asleep, both Lucy and the cider were getting cold, and I was regretting having eaten three whoopie pies. "Ready to head back?" I whispered.

"Ssshhh." Charlene put a hand on my arm. "Over there."

As I peered through the scrim of bushes separating us from Henry's glowing pumpkin tent, something caught my eye. A light, bobbing along near the ground.

"I didn't know ghosts carried flashlights," I whispered.

Charlene whacked me lightly on the arm. "It's not a flashlight," she hissed.

She was right, I realized as it hovered close to the glowing tent. I strained to see if I could catch a glimpse of a person, but the bobbing light disappeared behind the tent seemingly on its own.

"What do we do now?" Charlene asked when it didn't reappear after a minute or two.

"Call Ghostbusters?" I quipped, but something about it creeped me out. We waited a long time, but the light didn't reappear.

"Let's go check it out," Lucy whispered.

I turned to look at my old college roommate. "You, too?"

"If anything, it will keep my feet from freezing off. Remember, I'm used to Texas, not Maine," she said.

"What if they come back?" I asked.

"Then we say hi," Charlene said. "Come on."

I followed my intrepid friends over to where the lights had been bobbing. "There are footprints," Charlene said, looking at where the ground was lit by the greenhouse.

"Probably Henry Hoyle coming to check on his prize pumpkin," I pointed out. I peeked into the greenhouse. Henry's pumpkin was an absolute monster; whatever he was doing seemed to be working. "You could fit Cinderella and both of her stepsisters in that thing," I said.

"The leaves are looking a little yellow, though, don't you think?" Lucy asked. "It doesn't look like mosaic virus."

"How do you know about mosaic virus?" I asked.

"I'm supposed to know about things like mosaic virus. I'm thinking of buying a farm, remember?" she asked. Lucy's grandmother's old farm had recently come up for sale in Buttercup, Texas, and she was considering quitting her job and buying it. I was all for it, but she was still on the fence.

"The footsteps go into the woods, though," Charlene said. "And his house is over there," she said, pointing to where the windows glowed a hundred yards away.

"And the lights moved away from the house," Charlene pointed out.

"I thought you said it was a ghost." "I said it could be," she said.

Charlene's eyes glinted. "Maybe it's the ghost who keeps messing with the corn maze."

"Don't remind me," I groaned. The town council had grown a big field of corn for a fall corn maze, and I'd spent half of the last week helping him cut down stray stalks and putting in destination markers. Unfortunately, someone seemed to think it was fun to relocate them for me. So far, they'd turned up at the lighthouse, the general store, and Marge O'Leary's chicken coop.

"At least you got out of judging this time," she pointed out.

"It was a stroke of genius to say I wanted to be a contestant instead of a judge," I agreed. Last time I'd agreed to judge an island cooking contest, it had taken me six months to soothe the hurt feelings. "Gertrude Pickens is already unpopular; she can't do herself any more damage." The local *Daily Mail* reporter was not an island favorite. I turned to Lucy. "If you do move to Buttercup, don't agree to judge any cooking contests."

"I promise," Lucy said, and peered into the greenhouse. "Wow. That really is an enormous pumpkin. I see he's using the sugar-water trick."

"What's that?" I asked.

"See how there's a slit in the stem, and a wick going into it?" she asked. I looked; there was a wick leading from a gallon jug and feeding into the stem. "What does that do?"

"The sugar water helps it grow bigger," she said.

"It's maple syrup, I hear."

"Same concept," she said. "You do that the last few weeks before harvest."

"I wonder if that's what Phoebe McAlister is doing, too," Charlene wondered.

"Who's Phoebe McAlister?" Lucy asked.

"She's on the east side of the island, and apparently is growing a monster of her own," I said.

"Competition is supposed to be fierce this year," Charlene told her. "Henry and Phoebe have been duking it out for years; this is the first time Henry thinks he really has a shot at the title."

"I'll say," Lucy said. "I just hope it makes it that long... it looks a little... saggy."

"What do you mean?" Charlene asked.

"Look," she said, pointing to the top of the pumpkin. Lucy was right; it did seem a bit wrinkled around the stem.

"I thought pumpkins were supposed to last for months," I said.

"Maybe it's diseased, or something. But I can't think what it would be."

As she spoke, the lights flickered in the distance again. "Wait a moment," I said. "That's right by the corn maze!"

"Something tells me it's not a ghost," I said. "Let's go!"

Together, we hurried through the woods. By the time we reached the maze, though, the lights had vanished.

"I don't see anything out of place, do you?" Charlene asked, scanning the maze with her flashlight.

"Do you think they're in the maze?"

"I'm guessing they've done what they came to do," she said, training her lights on the entrance. I gasped.

"Is that blood?" Lucy asked in a low voice, looking at the dark red liquid that had been splattered all over the corn stalks flanking the entrance.

"It sure isn't hot chocolate," I said.

"It looks like someone was murdered," Lucy breathed.

"What's that?" Charlene said, her light focusing on a reddish lump near the entrance.

I took a few steps forward. "I... I think it's a heart," I said.

Lucy's hand leapt to her throat. "You don't think it's..."

"Human?" Charlene said. "I sure hope not, but I think it may be time to call John."

∾

"I don't know how you do it, Nat," John said later that night, when we were back in the kitchen at the Gray Whale Inn. Lucy had gone up to bed, and my handsome fiancé, the island deputy, had just gotten off the phone with the mainland police.

I cradled a mug of tea in my hands; I was still chilled. "Do what?"

"Find trouble," John said.

"Charlene wanted to see the ghost," I said. "We were trying to make a fun night of it." I sipped my tea. "What's the verdict?"

"We're supposed to keep it in the freezer," he said, "but the coroner says it's a pig heart."

"That's a relief," I said, slumping back.

"And the blood?"

"I'll send the sample over tomorrow," he said.

"What about the festival?"

"I took pictures and samples; I got the okay to clean things up for tomorrow."

"I guess blood on the corn maze is a little too ghoulish for the kids," I said. "Even though it is almost Halloween."

"I don't understand who would do something like that, though," he said. "I mean, what's the benefit?"

"You don't think it's teenagers having a lark?" I asked.

"Maybe," he said. "But I know all the teenagers here. I can't think who would be responsible." He sighed. "There was a message, too."

"I didn't see that."

"It was written in blood inside the maze."

"And?" I said, taking another sip of tea.

"It said 'cursed land,'" he told me.

"Well, there is supposed to be an Indian burial ground near there," I said. "Remember that shell midden someone found?"

"That's essentially a Native American trash heap, not a burial ground," he pointed out. "Besides, I don't think the Abenaki spoke English."

"I wouldn't want to build a house there, even so." I shivered, thinking of the ghost that had turned up in my own kitchen a few years back. I hadn't seen her since, but it had been unsettling to say the least.

"Well, there's going to be one whether there's a ghost or not.."

"It's such a shame," I said. It was a beautiful meadow, and the location of the annual Cranberry Island Pumpkin Patch and Harvest Festival for years. "You think someone's trying to convince Eileen's family not to sell?"

"By splashing the corn maze with blood and writing weird symbols on the ground?'" John grabbed a molasses crackle cookie from the jar. "I doubt it. Eileen's kids aren't even in Maine; they live down in Connecticut these days. It's probably just Halloween hijinks," he said.

"We saw somebody by Henry's greenhouse, too,"

I said. "And Lucy said the pumpkin looks like it's in trouble."

"Because it's so enormous it's imploding?"

"No... it looks like it's diseased—at least that's what Lucy thinks."

"That'll be a disappointment for him," John said. "But Phoebe will be thrilled. He was talking about cheating down at the store the other day... thinks she is pumping it full of Human Growth Hormone."

"How is that going to help a pumpkin grow?"

"I don't know, but he looked like he was about to commit pumpkin murder the other day down at the store. Henry's wife Emmeline was there, too."

"Did she say anything?"

"I got the feeling she was looking forward to the judging being over."

I laughed. "It's never dull here on Cranberry Island, is it?"

"Not with you around, it isn't," he said, and pulled me into an embrace that made me forget all about what we'd found at the corn maze.

∼

By the time Lucy and I got to the festival the next afternoon, the blood had been cleaned up and everything was looking autumnal and beautiful.

The backdrop of dark green evergreens mixed with yellow birch and red maples was stunning, and the sky was a clear, crystalline blue. I caught a whiff of wood smoke, and the buzz of excited voices added a festive air. Many families had come over from the mainland for the day, and the pumpkin patch was doing a booming business. Charlene was doing a brisk business selling hot cider and sugared donuts, along with some molasses crackle cookies I had made. The smell of spiced cider mixed with the fall was intoxicating.

"Want me to take over for a bit?" I asked Charlene when there was a break in the line at the wooden stall she had put up near the judging tent.

"No," she said. "I'm too busy grilling people."

"Find anything out?"

"Well, I'm not the only one who's seen the lights," she said. "And apparently," she added in a lower voice, "I'm not the only one who thinks the place is haunted."

Before I could ask more, there was a loud voice from across the pumpkin patch.

"You poisoned my pumpkin!"

I turned to look; it was Henry, confronting Phoebe. Next to him, in a wheelbarrow, was his pumpkin—or what was left of it. If it had looked a little mushy last night, today it looked more like pumpkin puree... only slimier.

"I did no such thing, and I resent the implication, sir!" responded Phoebe, drawing herself up to her full 5'3".

"I'm going to get to the bottom of this," Henry fumed. "I'm going to find out how you did it, and then I'm going to get my revenge." His face was a deep purple. Behind him, looking slightly embarrassed, was his wife, Emmeline. I shot her a sympathetic look, and she rolled her eyes. "Henry," she said, reaching for his arm, but he brushed her off.

"Somebody better go separate them, or Henry is going to have a heart attack," Charlene said.

"If he doesn't smother Phoebe with rotten pumpkin."

As if he'd heard us, Tom Lockhart, president of the lobster co-op, stepped up to the two gardeners. "What's going on here?" he asked.

"This woman sabotaged my garden," Henry said, stabbing a finger at Phoebe. "Look at this pumpkin. Two days ago, it was glorious. Then someone salted my maple water, and now look at it!"

"Saltwater," Lucy breathed. "That's what it was."

"Looks like we should have brought John," I commented. "If they don't cool off, we might need a deputy in a moment."

"Let me get this straight," Tom said, one hand on Henry's shoulder. "You think Phoebe sabotaged your pumpkin?"

"I'm sure of it," Henry said. "Someone put salt and vinegar in the sugar solution I was using… and now, four months of work are down the toilet. Would you want to eat pie made with that?" he asked, pointing at the pile of orange flesh.

"What makes you think Phoebe was responsible?"

"Who else would have a reason? She knew my pumpkin was going to squash hers, so she squashed mine."

"How dare you accuse me of that!" Phoebe shot back. "I had nothing to do with your pumpkin's untimely demise. Besides which, isn't it cheating to pump sugar water into your pumpkin?"

"It wasn't pumped," he said. "And it's perfectly legal. It was extra nutrition, delivered through the stem…"

"I still think it's dirty pool," Phoebe sniffed.

"It doesn't matter now," Tom pointed out. "Why don't we just keep moving?"

"We need Deputy Quinton to look into it," Henry fumed, invoking my fiancé.

"I promise I'll ask him to look into it," Tom said. "In the meantime, let's just go our separate ways, okay?"

"Since I don't have a pumpkin for the contest, I might as well go home," Henry said.

"Don't you want a donut?" Emmeline asked.

"No," he said, wheeling his wheelbarrow around and stomping off the grounds. Emmeline watched him go, then shrugged and walked over to the donut line.

"She doesn't look too broken up about the pumpkin contest," Lucy observed.

"I think she's been a pumpkin widow for two months," I said. "Donuts sound good; let's go get one."

We followed Emmeline to the back of the line. She smiled when she saw me, and I introduced her to Lucy. "Emmeline's responsible for that banana bread recipe I used on Monday," I told Lucy.

"That was your recipe?" Lucy asked. "I'm impressed."

"Thanks," Emmeline said with a smile. "No pumpkin bread for me this year, though."

"I heard," I said, looking toward where Henry had stalked away with the wheelbarrow. "Sorry about that!"

She waved my condolences away. "Oh, don't worry about it. He was obsessed with it anyway. Maybe now he can get back to normal." She turned to Lucy. "What brings you up to Cranberry Island?"

"Visiting Natalie, of course," she said. "And trying to decide whether to quit my job and sign my life away, actually."

"Oh?" Emmeline said, her dark eyes bright. "In what way?"

"Her grandmother's farm just came up for sale in Texas," I explained to Emmeline. "She's trying to decide whether or not she should quit her job in Houston and set herself up as a homesteader."

Emmeline studied her. "What do you really want to do?"

"I think I want to do it. But I also think I'm crazy."

I laughed. "I totally get it," I told her. "I went through the same thing when I bought the inn."

"Buy it," Emmeline said. "You only live once, you know? Don't want to die with regrets."

I looked at my friend. "Told you so," I said as Emmeline ordered herself two cider donuts.

"What do I do if the farm fails?" she asks.

"Come help me with reservations and breakfast," I told her with a grin. "But it won't fail. You'll be fine." I glanced over at the corn maze. "Want to try it?" I asked.

"Donuts first," she said. "We'll need our strength!"

∼

We ate our donuts and walked around the pumpkin patch, which was being staffed by the few high school students on Cranberry Island.

"How's it going?" I asked Emily Flowers, who was in line to be valedictorian at Mount Desert Island High School and planning to be a marine biologist.

"It's going okay," she said, but she didn't look happy.

"What's wrong?" I asked.

She pulled on a strand of her long, dark hair. "It's just sad that this is the last year we'll get to have it here. I've been coming to this festival my whole life."

"Yeah," said her friend Kitty. "They take our field so they can build a giant house and come out to the island for two weeks out of the year, when this has been a part of our community for our whole lives. It isn't fair."

"No, it's not," I said. "I have to agree with you."

"There's no way to stop it?" Lucy asked.

"I'm hoping we can maybe do something during the permitting phase," I said. "We couldn't raise the funds to buy the property, but we're still trying."

"Well, we're not going down without a fight," Emily said, thrusting out her chin.

"I admire your passion," I said. Maybe there was hope. After all, I'd managed to keep the inn from becoming a parking lot a few years ago. "If there's anything I can do to help out, let me know."

"I think we have it under control," Kitty said. Emily stepped on her foot, and she yelped.

"Come on," her friend said. "We have to go, remember?"

She glanced at her watch. "Oh, yeah. Nice talking to you," she said, giving me a quick smile and following her friend toward the back of the pumpkin patch.

"I hope they pull it off," Lucy said.

"Me too," I said. "In the meantime, ready to tackle the maze?"

"After you," she told me, popping the last bit of donut into her mouth and licking her fingers. There was only a smudge of rusty red at the base of the hay bales marking the entrance to the maze, which we decided to attempt now that we were fortified with a few of Charlene's amazing donuts. The goal was to find five different targets—and then find our way out.

"I guess this is the last year for this," Lucy said, still licking her fingers as we started down one of the pathways.

"It will be if the property sells," I said.

"I hope it doesn't," she told me. "This is what I always imagined Halloween should be like. The pumpkins, the fall air, the corn maze…" Her cheeks were pink. "Maybe I can do something like this at Dewberry Farm!"

"You've named it?" I asked.

She blushed a deeper shade of pink. "It's what I used to call it as a child," she said.

"Your heart is there, isn't it?" I asked.

"My heart is," she admitted. "But my head is telling me I'm crazy."

I laughed. "I totally understand. When I told my financial advisor what I was planning on doing, he told me I'd be in the soup line within a year."

"Encouraging," Lucy said.

"Yes. I didn't sleep for a week."

"But it all worked out, didn't it?"

"So far, so good," I agreed. We turned right, and then left, going deeper into the maze. As we moved further into the field, the sounds of the festival faded, replaced by the rustling of the dried corn stalks. It was almost eerie, somehow.

"It's a lot bigger than I thought," Lucy said. "What are we looking for again?"

"A pumpkin, a witch, a ghost, and a zombie," I reminded her.

"How could I forget?"

We traipsed on a while longer, taking random

turns. "This is a huge piece of property," Lucy said. "They want all this for a house?"

"It's got a great view of the water," I said. "But it will be sad to lose the location of the harvest festival."

"Can't the island council do something to prevent it?"

"We're trying," I said, "but unless we can pool enough money to buy the property, I'm afraid we're out of luck."

"I can't believe an islander's children are selling the property," she said.

I sighed. "They lost touch with the island a long time ago. And I suppose it would be hard to turn down three quarters of a million dollars."

"That much? Ouch."

"Exactly," I said. "Which is why this is the last year."

There was a popping sound from somewhere nearby. "What was that?"

"Sounded like firecrackers," Lucy said. "Or maybe a cap gun."

As we walked farther, there was a crackling sound from the corn stalk to our left.

We rounded a bend, and the crackling of the dried corn stalks got louder.

"It smells like someone's lit a fire already," Lucy

said. "It's not that cold, is it?"

"It doesn't smell like wood burning," I pointed out. "And it's awfully close.

I stopped suddenly as we turned a corner. Lucy stifled a scream.

There was a wall of fire in front of us, and it was headed our way.

∽

"Fire!" I yelled as we plunged through the dried cornstalks, no longer paying any attention to the pathways. Had anyone been caught in the flames? "Fire!" Lucy yelled beside me. I hazarded a glance behind me; I couldn't see the flames anymore, but I could smell smoke. I just hoped the wind wouldn't push the fire in our direction.

"How big is this thing?" Lucy asked as we plunged through yet another line of cornstalks. Lorraine Lockhart and her daughter, Meredith, were looking wide-eyed in the next corridor.

"We have to get out of here," I told Lorraine. "The maze is on fire."

She instinctively clutched her daughter to her chest, then released her and said, "Let's go." She joined us calling "Fire" as we pushed through the maze, trampling on the paper witch that was supposed to be a prize. Lucy led the way, followed by Lorraine and Meredith; I brought up the rear. The rows went on and on, and the crackling sound grew nearer and nearer. I prayed we would make it out in time – and that everyone else, would, too.

Finally, we burst through into the meadow.

"Did everyone get out?" I asked. "Are they getting the fire truck?"

"It's already here," Lorraine said, pointing to Eleazer Spurrell, who was spraying the fire. It looked like he was trying to put out a grill with a mister.

"If you're in the maze, come this way!" I yelled, hoping anyone who was still in there could hear me. "Just go through the stalks and come toward our voices."

"Where are you?" a voice called.

I felt as if I'd been dashed with ice water. The fire was racing our direction. Could we find the person in the maze in time?

"I'm right here," I said. "Keep talking; I'll come toward you."

Lucy grabbed my arm. "Nat…"

"I can't leave someone in there."

"Then I'm coming with you," she said.

Together we plunged back into the maze, still

calling. The flames were getting closer... and we were moving toward them.

"Where are you?" called the voice, which was sounding more panicky. It was to our left; I took a sharp turn, pushing the dried stalks out of my way as I battered through another wall.

It was Claudette White and her grandson, Jacob, looking terrified.

"This way," I said, reaching for Claudette's hand. I knew she had sprained an ankle recently; she was wearing a clunky boot that made walking laborious.

"Can I pick you up?" Lucy asked the little boy. "We'll go faster that way."

The flames raced toward us as he reached his chubby arms up.

"Go first," I told Lucy.

"How far is it?" Claudette asked as I helped her through the battered corn stalks.

"Not far," I said. It wasn't, but the fire was advancing fast. Would we make it in time?

Lucy and Jacob raced ahead as Claudette stopped to lift her clunky boot over a broken stalk. I started to sweat; I could feel the heat from the fire behind us.

"Go without me," Claudette said.

"No," I said. "No way. Lean on me," I said. "We'll do it like a three-legged race." I didn't wait for her to agree; I just put my arm around her and plunged ahead, pulling her along with me.

Adrenaline pulsed through me. The flames roared behind us as I pulled Claudette through the dried cornstalks, praying we'd make it in time. Finally, we burst through the last wall of cornstalks, smoke burning our lungs.

"Grandma!" Jacob hurled himself into Claudette's arms.

"Is everyone else out?" I asked.

"I hope so," Lucy said, and we both turned and watched as the fire devoured the rest of the corn maze. Emily and Kitty, the two high school girls we had talked with stood nearby, looking pale and stricken. Another piece of their childhood gone up in smoke, I reflected grimly.

"I wish there was something else we could do," Lucy said.

"I know. I'm just glad it rained last night. It's not spreading beyond the maze."

"Thank goodness," Lucy said, looking around at the houses. "Everything on this island is built of wood."

"I just hope there was no one else in there," I said, shuddering.

As I said it, Emily let out a sob, looking horrified, and I wished I'd kept my mouth shut.

∽

It took about an hour for the fire to die down; the volunteer firefighters concentrated on keeping the edges under control, making sure it didn't leap across to the nearby woods. Miraculously, no one was unaccounted for; except for a minor burn on Claudette's ankle, everyone had escaped unscathed.

"What do you think caused it?" I asked Eleazer.

"We found what look like some firecrackers toward the side of the maze," he told me. "They probably caught the dry stalks on fire."

"At least it doesn't sound like it was intentional. Lucy and I heard some popping noises before it started," I told him.

"Probably just pranksters. Dangerous prank, though; I'm glad nobody was seriously hurt." Or died, I knew he was thinking.

As he walked back to help fold up the hose, someone spoke behind me. "I think they're right; this land is cursed." I turned to see Marge O'Leary talking with a woman I didn't recognize.

"I heard there was an Indian burial ground here," the woman responded in an ominous tone. "Maybe they're not happy about the building being put up. Did you hear about the blood on the corn maze?"

"I heard there was a heart, too," Marge said.

"They shouldn't build on this land. That's the reason old Eileen didn't build a house here—that's why it's been empty so long."

I glanced at Lucy, whose eyebrows lifted, as they drifted away.

"I know Charlene was talking about a ghost, but firecrackers and a pig heart don't exactly sound supernatural to me," I murmured.

"Me neither," she said as Charlene hurried over to us, looking worried. "Claudette's going to be okay, thankfully; I'm so glad you two helped her and her grandson out of there. Any word on what started it?"

"Firecrackers, they think," I reported. "Pranksters, probably."

"Well, it's sad to lose the corn maze, but I guess this was the last year anyway." Charlene pulled a long face. "I'm just glad nobody got caught in it."

"Are they still going to do the pumpkin judging and the baking contest?"

"They're on the schedule for tomorrow," she said.

"If Phoebe's pumpkin makes it that far. Henry looked like he was about to commit vegetablecide."

"Who knew harvest festivals could be so full of drama?"

"You have no idea," Charlene said, shaking her head.

"Wait until the baking competition tomorrow," I

said. "I got roped into judging last year… never again."

"That bad?"

Charlene grimaced. "I think I stopped one of the library volunteers from taking a contract out on Nat—but only barely."

"Maybe I shouldn't move to a small town," Lucy quipped. "It might be safer in the city."

∽

Lucy joined me in the kitchen that night as I assembled the final version of my Turtle Pumpkin Pie. I had chilled the pie dough earlier in the day; now, as my friend sat across from me, I rolled out the dough and formed it in the pie pan.

"My grandmother used to make pies," Lucy said, pushing a loose strand of brown hair out of her face. She had the same round, sunny face she'd had when we were in college almost twenty years ago. "One of my best memories is sitting in the kitchen while she made a peach pie in early summer.

"I do miss the peaches sometimes," I said. "But I don't miss summers."

"No," she agreed. "But at least I don't have to shovel the driveway."

I finished crimping the edges of the pie dough

and looked up at her. "Do you think you're going to buy the farm?"

"It's financially a huge risk," she said. "But it's something I've always wanted to do, and I just don't want to wait and then find out I waited too long. Besides, it's my grandmother's farm. This may be my only chance." She sipped her hot cider. "I kind of thought you were crazy when you quit and moved up here, after taking one trip."

I grinned. "I did, too, to be honest. I had a lot of sleepless nights."

"And now?"

"And now, I can't imagine living any other way," I said as I put the finishing touches on the crust and turned the oven on. "No commute, no boss, no bureaucracy… it's amazing. There is bookkeeping," I said, "and keeping reservations straight, but it's definitely worth it."

"I'll bet," she said, and I could tell by the look on her face that she was imagining waking up in her grandmother's farm. "The thing is, though, I've been gardening for years, but it's different having your own garden than growing crops to sell."

"A lot of people here do crafts, too," I suggested. "Candles, soaps… you can grow flowers. Diversify. Have you visited any other small farms?"

"A few," she said. "It looked doable."

I dumped a can of pumpkin into a bowl and measured out half and half. "What do they think?"

"They say it's hard work, but it's worth it."

I added sugar to the bowl. "Can you make the numbers work with your savings?"

"I can," she said. "Barely, but I can." "Then what do you have to lose?"

"Other than my life savings?" she grinned.

"You can always sell it if it doesn't work out," I said. "But I suspect that won't happen."

"You're a bad influence, you know," she said.

"Bad?" I grinned. "Or good? Can you zest a lemon for me?" I asked.

"I thought you'd never ask," she said, as I tossed her a lemon. "The zester's in the middle drawer," I said, pointing to it.

"In the meantime," she asked, "what do you think is going on at the festival?"

"I think someone's trying to scare off the buyer, if you ask me," I said. "Did you hear that conversation about the place being haunted?'

"Sounds pretty far-fetched to me," she said. "Although it would explain the lights at night."

"But the lights have been there for weeks," I said, "and the pig heart didn't turn up until this morning."

"Maybe someone's pretending to be a ghost?" "Maybe," I said, but I wasn't convinced. "I think something else is going on."

"Should we go and check it out tonight?" she asked as she rinsed the lemon in the sink.

"John won't be happy," I said.

"He can come with us," she suggested.

"Let's get the pie done and we'll go look," I told her. "We saw lights in the woods, right?"

She nodded. "Maybe they'll turn up again. In which case, it might be a good idea to have John with us."

I finished mixing in the sugar and the spices, and Lucy added the lemon zest. "All we need to do now is put together the topping," I said.

"I'll do the rest," Lucy said, looking at my recipe. "Go check with John."

"Thanks," I said as she scanned the recipe and reached for the pecans. We'd spent half our college days baking; my future mother-in-law was a disaster in the kitchen, but anything Lucy turned her hand to came out delicious. "I'll be back in a few," I said, and untied my apron.

～

By the time John and I stepped back into the kitchen, the smell of pumpkin pie was wafting through the kitchen. "Are you sure we have to give that to the judges?" John asked.

"There's a little of the sample pie still in the fridge," I said. "And there are a few whoopie pies left, too."

"Tough decision," he said. "But I think I'll go for the pie."

"So," Lucy said, grinning at John as he opened the fridge. "Did she talk you into it?"

"Well, if I said no, I know you two would go on your own, so I suppose that's a yes," he said. "And there's always the chance that whoever is responsible will come back, so it's not a bad idea."

"Excellent," I said. "Pie will be done in ten minutes, and then we're good to go."

"I'm going to run upstairs and put on something warmer," Lucy said. "Back in a few!"

∽

It was almost fully dark when we walked over to the meadow where the Harvest Festival took place. "Still smells like smoke," Lucy commented.

"It probably will for a while, unfortunately," I said, as we stopped to survey the area.

"No lights yet," John observed. "Where did you see them?'

"Over by the trees," I told him, and together we skirted the blackened field and headed for the trees.

"This way," I said, pointing to the right. He flashed his light on the ground. "Boot prints," he said.

"There were a lot of people here today," I pointed out.

"Not in the trees, though. This might have something to do with the lights."

We walked a bit further and discovered a large brown tarp covered over with dead leaves and vegetation. "What is this?" I asked.

John bent down and lifted a corner of the tarp, revealing a grid marked out with posts and plastic tape.

"Looks like a scientific survey of some sort," he said.

"Only it's been dug out," I replied, looking at the square holes in the ground. "Like someone's looking for something."

"Maybe Indian artifacts?" Lucy asked.

"It's a good thought—and it's on a bit of a hillock," I said. "But if they are, why be secret about it?"

"Maybe because the land doesn't belong to whoever's conducting the survey," John said.

"You think this has something to do with the

burial ground that's rumored to be here?"

"If someone found one, that might scuttle the sale," Lucy said.

"You think?" I asked.

"If you can show that it's a site of archeological importance, then there are often prohibitions about building."

"Interesting," I said. "Maybe we should wait a while and see if someone turns up."

"You think they will?"

"You saw lights last night, didn't you?" John asked. "Yes, but I think those were at the corn maze. Still," I said, "I guess the pie is done, and there's no one at the inn but us... why not?" I asked.

Together, the three of us walked a ways into the woods until we found a fallen log that was shielded by a few low bushes.

"I wish we'd brought more of those whoopie pies," Lucy grumbled after we'd been sitting in silence for twenty minutes.

"Me too," I whispered, and John shushed me. I caught a glimpse of a flashlight bobbing through the trees, moving in our direction. Before long, there was a crack of a breaking branch, and low voices drifted over to us.

"... set the fire?"

"Don't know." The first voice was male, and the

second voice was female—I didn't recognize either of them. A few moments later, I heard another fragment of conversation... "find the site?"

"It doesn't look disturbed." We heard the sound of the tarp being lifted. "Do you think we have enough?"

"I think so," the female voice said. "But a bone fragment would be ideal."

"Fingers crossed," the man responded.

We sat on the log for two hours while they worked... it was obviously an archeological dig. My leg kept falling asleep, and the log was becoming very uncomfortable. I was about to propose we go home when there was a stifled whoop from the mystery pair.

"I've got something."

"What is it?"

"A femur, I think," the woman said.

A minute later, the man concurred. There was a series of flashes—pictures, I surmised. A few minutes later, I heard the sound of the tarp being replaced, and the lights began moving away.

"Let's follow them," I whispered.

"Let's wait until they're under way, first," John said. "I'll go first."

A few minutes later, we followed the bobbing lights through the trees. I was thankful for the little light the moon provided; it wasn't terrific, but it did spare me from tripping over as many branches. It wasn't far to the road, and we followed them as they turned onto a long driveway I recognized.

"That's Murray Selfridge's house," I whispered.

"Who's that?" Lucy asked.

"My mother's boyfriend," John answered, watching as the lights disappeared into the garage. "I think we have a few questions to ask her when we get home."

∼

Catherine was still up when we knocked on the door to the carriage house.

"What's up?" she asked, wrapping her bathrobe around her.

"Sorry to bother you," I said. "But we have a question... does Murray have house guests?" John asked.

"He does, actually," she said. "He's hosting some students from the University of Maine. Why?"

"Do you know why they're here?"

"Some sort of research." She shrugged a satin-clad shoulder. "I never asked."

"Did he say if it was archeological?" John asked.

"He never said. Why?"

"I think they're digging on Eileen's land in secret," I told her.

A furrow appeared between her eyebrows. "Why on earth would they do that?"

"That's what we'd like to know," John said. "Would you ask him?"

"Why don't you ask him?" she replied.

"I'm guessing you're more likely to get the real answer," John said with a grin.

She grinned back. "Okay," she said. "I'll ask tomorrow. But he may not tell me... he likes to surprise me sometimes."

"Oh, I'll bet you can get it out of him," John teased her.

She turned a light shade of pink. "Isn't it past your bedtime, young man?"

He laughed. "Let us know what you find out," he said, and we headed back up to the inn together.

∽

"It's an archeological dig," Catherine told me the next morning, just as I was finishing up the breakfast dishes. "But I'm not supposed to say anything about it."

"I wonder what he's up to?" I asked.

"He says he's doing a good deed," she said. "You

must be a good influence on him," I told my future mother-in-law with a smile. I thought about what Lucy had said about archeological finds. Was it possible that Murray secretly hired a team of archeologists to find evidence that would prevent the land from being developed? I never thought I'd find Murray, who had spent the last twenty years trying to turn the island into a posh resort, trying to prevent someone from building, but if I was right, I had to hand it to him. I was hoping last night's discovery would be enough to stop the sale of the property... or at least lower the price enough so that we could raise the money to buy it for the town.

"What do you think it is he's doing?" Catherine asked, fingering the pearls around her neck.

"I'll let you know when I'm sure," I told her. "But if I'm right, I'm cooking him dinner."

She sighed. "Nobody tells me anything!"

~

The festival was already in full swing when Lucy and I arrived at noon. I'd dropped my pie off at eight. There were several other delicious-looking offerings—with the exception of Claudette's, which I knew had contained no sugar and recognized by the crust, which looked like it was made of Play-Doh—

but it looked like no one else had thought to use pecans. I thought of them as my secret Southern weapon.

A very full-looking Gertrude Pickens was slipping a few Tums into her mouth when I got to the pie-judging tent. "Did you pick a winner?" I asked.

"I did," she groaned. "But I won't be able to eat for a week."

"I always say that," I said, "but it never works out that way."

Charlene was at the donut booth. When there was a lull in the line, I told her what we'd seen the night before—and what Catherine had told me about Murray.

"Do you think it's possible he's doing a good deed?" "I think he is," I said.

"Even if he does scuttle the sale, though," she said, "there's no way we can raise the money to afford the property."

"I guess it depends on how much they sell it for." I glanced back at the blackened earth where the corn maze once was. "And it still doesn't solve the issue of who put that heart by the maze—or set it on fire."

"I think I have at least an idea on the heart," Charlene said.

"What do you mean?"

"They were dissecting pig hearts in A.P. Biology

at the high school last week," she said. "Emily Flowers was telling Tania about it."

A.P. Biology. I looked over at the pumpkin patch, and everything clicked. "I'll be right back," I said.

"What's wrong?"

"Nothing's wrong. I just want to ask someone some questions," I said, and before Charlene could pry further, I drifted off toward the pumpkin patch.

The person I wanted to talk to was standing at the cash box, sorting bills. I walked over and smiled.

"Can I help you?" she asked.

"Yes," I said, looking around to make sure we were alone. "I know you're responsible for the pig heart," I said in a quiet voice. Her eyes widened. "And the firecrackers—I know you didn't mean to set the maze on fire. You were trying to make the property look haunted, or cursed, to scare off buyers."

Emily blanched. "How did you... I mean, I don't know what you're talking about!"

"You got the pig heart from your biology class." She clapped a hand to her mouth.

"Emily, I know how much this festival means to you," I said. "I won't say anything to anyone... but don't do anything else, okay? We got really lucky with the corn maze."

Tears filled her eyes. "I never meant to burn it down. I was so scared someone got hurt... or worse."

"I know," I said. "Someone else has been working behind the scenes—with any luck, the sale won't go through."

"Really?"

"I'm not a hundred percent sure, but I'm guessing we'll know in the next day or two."

"Oh, that would be so awesome."

"Don't say anything to anyone," I warned her. "And no more pranks, okay?"

"Okay."

"Promise?"

"Promise," she said. "Thank you," she added. "For talking to me—and for not saying anything."

"No worries, Emily," I said. As I spoke, the PA system crackled to life; it was time to announce the judges' results. "I've got to go hear if my pie won," I told her as I headed over to the tent. "We're all good?"

She nodded, looking relieved.

∽

Quite a crowd had gathered—primarily locals—to hear our selectman and Lobster Co-op president announce the results of the contests. I noticed Claudette White, in a sweater she'd knitted from wool she'd harvested and spun herself, looking hopeful that her sugar-free pie might take home a ribbon. Emmeline was there, too, in an orange dress with dangling pumpkin earrings, standing by her husband Henry, who was still looking apoplectic about his failed pumpkin. Although I didn't know what Emmeline had concocted for the pie competition, I knew whatever she'd made was going to be hard to beat.

The announcements started promptly at noon. The sun was high in the sky, and despite the blackened field that had been the corn maze, there was still a festive atmosphere.

The pumpkin contest was first. The contestants' pumpkins were lined up on hay bales, and there was no question who the winner was; Phoebe's pumpkin looked like Cinderella's Carriage lined up next to a bunch of Snow White's dwarves.

Emmeline stood beside Henry, who was actively fuming, while Phoebe stood behind her monstrous pumpkin, a thin-lipped, superior smile on her face.

Tom Lockhart, who had the bad luck to be in charge of distributing the awards, stepped up to the makeshift podium to distribute third and second prizes, and then, to no one's surprise, announced Phoebe the winner. "Let's have a round of applause for Phoebe's pumpkin... weighing in at 96 pounds and breaking the record for the largest pumpkin ever grown on Cranberry Island!"

Gertrude Pickens of the Daily Mail prepared to snap a photo as Phoebe walked up to accept her ribbon, beaming with pride.

At this not unexpected news, Henry exploded, his face turning a dangerous shade of purple. "She's a cheater!" he blurted. "She poisoned my pumpkin with vinegar and salt!"

"I did no such thing, sir," Phoebe said. "And I resent the implication."

"If my pumpkin dies, yours deserves to die, too!" he yelled, pulling a meat mallet out from behind his back.

"Henry!" Emmeline caught his arm.

"Out of my way, Emmeline," he said. "My only regret is that I didn't do this before the awards were given out."

"It wasn't Phoebe who killed your pumpkin," she said.

He blinked. "Nonsense. She poisoned my sugar water. Now, get out of my way."

"Henry," she said, putting her hands on her hips. "I poisoned your pumpkin."

"I said, out of my…" Suddenly, her words seemed to sink in. "Wait. You… you poisoned Josephine?"

"It even has a name," Emmeline said. "Yes," she

said. "I poisoned Josephine. I was tired of being a pumpkin widow."

"What do you mean?"

"You've practically lived in that greenhouse since June," she said, pumpkin earrings swinging. "I'm tired of eating dinner in the greenhouse. I'm tired of hearing about 'Josephine.' I just want my husband back!"

"You killed my pumpkin?" he asked, looking like he was about to burst into tears.

"I'm sorry, Henry," she said. "But something had to be done."

Phoebe sniffed, looking superior, and for a moment, I had a desire to take the meat mallet and finish off what Henry had been about to do. But Tom Lockhart was moving on. "And now," he said, "the results of the baking contest." He was opening an envelope when Charlene came up and whispered something in his ear, looking gleeful.

"You're kidding me," he said.

She shook her head. "Just got word this morning."

"Before we get to the pie judging," he said, "I have some excellent news."

A murmur passed through the crowd.

"It looks like this won't be the last year we have the Harvest Festival here after all. It turns out we've been holding the festival on an important archeological site for all these years," he said.

There was a murmur in the crowd.

"Apparently the buyer has backed out… and there's a new one."

The murmuring got louder.

"Let's give a big round of applause to Murray Selfridge! He's just signed a contract to purchase the property."

Confused silence. I could tell everyone else was wondering what I would be thinking: was Murray buying the property any better?

"Not to build on," Tom reassured the islanders. "He plans to donate it to the island!"

Whoops broke out all around, along with applause. I glanced over at Emily; she looked absolutely elated. I winked at Catherine, who was standing beside Murray, and she grinned at me. I had to say one thing for Murray; he sure worked fast. I wasn't surprised to see Gertrude Pickens making a beeline for him; she was going to get quite a scoop today.

"And now," he said, "let's proceed to the final judging." I noticed Claudette stand a little straighter. "Third prize goes to Fred Winters," he said. "For his Pumpkin Custard pie."

"Really?" he asked, looking shocked. "It was my first try!"

There was applause as he took his ribbon.

"Second prize goes to Emmeline Hoyle," he said, "for her pumpkin chess pie."

"I should have put vinegar and salt in your pie," her husband said sourly. She gave him a light whack on the arm and went up to accept her ribbon.

"And first prize," he said, "goes to Natalie Barnes for her pumpkin caramel turtle pie!"

Lucy whooped beside me, and Charlene pumped her fist as I went up to have my photo snapped by Gertrude. Maybe, for once, I thought, she'd have something nice to say about me in the paper.

"Congratulations," she said, and a moment later, the flash blinded me.

∼

"I can't believe they're not going to build a house on the property!" Lucy said when we got back to the inn later that afternoon. I took the rest of my pie with me, after giving Gertrude a slice and promising to e-mail her the recipe.

"I know," I told her as I slid the pie onto the counter. "For the first time ever, I actually think I like Murray Selfridge."

"That was awfully clever of him. Not quite legal, maybe… but clever."

"That's Murray for you."

"At least it was in service of good. John's mother is a good influence on him," she said.

"That's what I told her."

"I just wish I knew who set fire to the corn maze—and put that heart by the entrance."

I shrugged. "I guess we'll never know. So," I said as I cut the last remaining slices of my Turtle Pumpkin Pie and handed one to Lucy, "that was an exciting day."

"And a successful one," she said. "I'm thrilled you won the pie contest!"

"You helped," I reminded her.

"I spread pecans and brown sugar on top of it and put it in the oven," she said. "That's hardly a contribution."

"Every little bit helps," I said, slicing myself a thin wedge of pie and levering it onto a plate. "What a day."

"No kidding," she said. "And I thought life in a small town would be slow!"

"It's anything but, I assure you," I said as I sat down across from her at my pine kitchen table. "Did you decide what to do about the farm?"

She took a deep breath. "I think I'm going to do

it," she said. "I feel like I'm absolutely crazy for saying it, but I just feel like… well, like if I don't, I'm going to spend the rest of my life regretting it."

"I think this calls for a toast," I said, popping a bottle of sparkling apple cider and pouring two glasses.

"To Dewberry Farm," I said.

"To the rescue of the Harvest Festival," she said. "And the success of the Gray Whale Inn," she added as we clinked our glasses, grins on both our faces.

Want to read more about Lucy and Dewberry Farm? Download your copy of Killer Jam, the first Dewberry Farm mystery, now!

CHARLENE'S PUMPKIN WHOOPIE PIES

INGREDIENTS

Cookies:

- 1 1/2 cups flour
- 1/2 teaspoon baking powder
- 1/2 teaspoon baking soda
- 1/2 teaspoon salt
- 1 teaspoon ground cinnamon
- 1/2 teaspoon ground ginger
- 1/4 teaspoon freshly grated nutmeg
- 1/4 teaspoon ground cloves
- 1 cup packed light brown sugar
- 1/2 cup vegetable oil
- 1 (15-ounce) can pumpkin
- 1 large egg

- 1 teaspoon pure vanilla extract

Filling:

- 6 ounces cream cheese, softened
- 3/4 stick unsalted butter, softened
- Pinch of salt
- 1 1/2 cups confectioners' sugar
- 1/2 teaspoon vanilla extract
- 1/2 teaspoon almond extract

DIRECTIONS

1. Preheat oven to 350 and line 2 large baking sheets with parchment paper. Whisk together flour, baking powder, soda, salt, and spices in a bowl. In a separate bowl, whisk together sugar, oil, pumpkin, egg, and vanilla. Stir in dry ingredients.
2. Using a 1-ounce ice cream scoop or a tablespoon, drop a scant scoop of batter or 2 scant tablespoons of batter onto a parchment-lined baking sheet to form 1 mound. Make 15 more mounds, arranging them 2 inches apart until baking sheet is

PUMPKIN PIED

full (you will have batter left over). Bake until cookies spring back when touched, 12 to 18 minutes. Transfer cookies to rack to cool, then form and bake remaining batter on the other parchment-lined sheet. You should have a total of 32 cookie-cakes.

3. While cookies are baking, beat cream cheese, butter, and salt in a bowl with an electric mixer until smooth. Add confectioners' sugar, vanilla, and almond extract and mix on low speed until smooth.

4. Chill filling until firm 30 minutes to 1 hour. When filling is cool enough to keep its shape, spread 1 heaping tablespoon of filling each on flat side of half the cooled cookies, then top with a second cookie. If necessary, chill whoopie pies just long enough to firm up filling again, about 30 minutes.

PRIZE-WINNING TURTLE PUMPKIN PIE

INGREDIENTS

- 2 eggs
- 1 (15 ounce) can pumpkin puree
- 1/2 cup half-and-half
- 3/4 cup sugar
- 1 tablespoon flour
- 1 teaspoon lemon zest
- 1/2 teaspoon vanilla extract
- 1/4 teaspoon salt
- 1/4 teaspoon ground cinnamon
- 1/4 teaspoon ground nutmeg
- 1/8 teaspoon ground allspice
- 1 9-inch prepared pie shell, either butter crust (below) or store-bought

PUMPKIN PIE

- 3/4 cup packed light brown sugar
- 1 cup chopped pecans
- 3 tablespoons butter

DIRECTIONS

Preheat oven to 375. Combine eggs, pumpkin, and half-and-half in a mixing bowl and beat until smooth. Stir in the sugar, flour, lemon zest, vanilla, salt, cinnamon, nutmeg, and allspice, then pour the pumpkin mixture into the prepared pie shell. Cover the edges of the pie with aluminum foil strips to prevent burning, and bake for 20 minutes. While pie is baking, mix the brown sugar, pecans, and butter together in a bowl until evenly blended. Carefully spoon over the top of the pie and continue baking the pie until the topping is golden and bubbly, and a knife inserted in the center comes out clean, about 20 minutes more. Cool on a wire rack.

BUTTERY PIE CRUST

INGREDIENTS

- 2 1/2 cups all purpose flour

- 1 tablespoon sugar
- 3/4 teaspoon salt
- 1 cup chilled, unsalted butter, cut into 1/2-inch cubes
- 6 tablespoons (more or less) ice water

DIRECTIONS

Combine flour, sugar, and salt in food processor, then add butter and pulse until coarse meal forms. Gradually blend in ice water, tablespoon by tablespoon, to form moist clumps. Gather dough into ball and divide in half. Form dough into 2 balls; flatten into disks. Wrap each in plastic; chill 2 hours or overnight. Makes two 9-inch deep- dish pie crusts.

ICED INN

ICED INN

"Whose idea was it to have a wedding in December, anyway?" Charlene asked as she peered out the kitchen window at the darkening sky.

"I think it's kind of romantic," I replied as I pulled a pan of gingerbread cookies out of the oven and set it on a cooling rack. It was mid-December, and my niece Gwen was getting married to local lobsterman Adam Thrackton in just a couple of days. The wedding was going to be at our little island church, with the reception at the Gray Whale Inn, catered by yours truly. I had family coming in from California, along with a cousin who had recently moved to Bangor, just a few hours west.

"If you consider being snowed in with no power roman- tic," Charlene quipped. "Isn't your sister supposed to be coming in today?"

"She is," I confirmed. Adam's parents were arriving, too, and would be staying at the inn. I hoped the families would get along.

"Bridget still on board with the wedding?" Charlene asked.

"Last time I talked to her she was," I said. My high-achieving sister Bridget hadn't been thrilled when she learned her daughter's "shipping magnate" fiancé was actually a lobsterman. He had a degree from Princeton, so that helped, but even though she'd been grudgingly supportive after her last visit, I suspected she was still struggling with the idea of her talented daughter working as an artist on a small Maine island with her lobsterman husband. "They fly into Portland this evening; she's renting a car and driving up."

"If they don't get diverted," Charlene said. "There's a storm rolling in; it's supposed to snow at least a foot over the next few days."

I glanced out the window at the approaching clouds as I transferred the warm cookies from the pan to the cooling rack. "As long as it holds off until they make it here, we'll be fine. We've got plenty of firewood, propane, and enough food to feed an army for a month."

"I may just stay here then," Charlene said.

"You're welcome to," I said as I retrieved another

ball of dough from the refrigerator and began rolling it out. As I worked, I inhaled a deep whiff of the warm, spicy scent that permeated my yellow kitchen. I'd decorated the inn for Christmas, with boughs of fresh greens on the mantle, wreaths--one of which was adding its balsam fragrance to the already deliciously scented kitchen--and a Christmas tree John and I had selected and cut down just the day before. He was busy on a last-minute order of toy boats for Island Artists, which had seen a holiday boom since starting an online ordering business, and I was busy getting ready for our guests. I'd made thumbprints, sugar cookies, and a batch of decadent caramel-fudge bars, but it wasn't the Christmas season for me without gingerbread. "You can stay anytime," I reiterated to Charlene, who seemed kind of glum. "We've got room."

"We'll see," she said, taking a sip of her hot chocolate and leaning her chin on one hand. "Romance is in the air right now, it seems. Even Marge O'Leary has a beau."

"What? I knew she broke her foot, but no one said anything about a beau."

"Frank Duggin is crazy about her," she said. "His boat's been having all kinds of troubles the last few months-- something with the fuel tank is the latest problem, I hear-- so he's been at the store more often than usual, and he's gotten to know her a bit. Now he's writing her bad poetry and leaving roses on her doorstep."

"Good for her," I said. Marge's romantic past had been less than idyllic--her ex-husband was currently in jail for murder--and I was glad something positive was going on in her personal life.

"Not really," Charlene says. "She wants nothing to do with him. She leaves the flowers and doesn't read the poetry. At least she says she doesn't." Charlene grimaced. "She says she'll never get married again."

"You don't have to marry someone just because you have dinner with him," I said. "Maybe she should at least give it a shot. He's a nice man."

"It would probably help his cause if he bathed more," Charlene mused. "He smells like a bait cooler at a filling station."

"Eau de Lobsterman," I quipped.

"Even so, I heard Anna Potts is incredibly jealous."

"Of Marge?"

"She's had her eye on Frank for years," Charlene said. "She thinks Marge broke her foot just to get his attention."

"And people say life on a small island is boring," I commented.

"I know, right?" She looked out the window at the

snowflakes spiraling down from the wintry sky and sighed. "Think I'll ever get married?"

I looked at my beautiful friend; her caramel-colored hair glowed in the afternoon light from the window, and her purple cardigan hugged her curvy form. Half the island's men would have given a limb to be married to Charlene, but she hadn't yet found anyone who floated her boat. There had more than a few false starts, the most recent being a naturalist who had visited the island for a summer tour and carried Charlene's heart away with him. Charlene had recently called it quits with him when she realized her dream of a full-time relationship wasn't going to be a possi- bility with a photographer who never spent more than a week in the same place. "I think you could have your pick," I told her honestly.

"Sadly, the selection isn't terrific. You and Gwen have skimmed the cream off the top of Cranberry Island."

Although I couldn't disagree with her--my husband John was amazing, and Gwen's intended was pretty awesome, too--I knew agreeing with her would be counter- productive. "The sea is bigger than just Cranberry Island," I reminded her. I'd been trying to get her to post an online dating profile for years. She'd talked of moving to Portland not long ago, and I was afraid to lose my closest friend. "I think you should broaden your search."

"Maybe," she said, finishing her hot chocolate and standing up. "I should probably head back to the store and close up." Charlene ran the island's only store (and post office); she had help, but she'd promised to let her niece Tania off early.

"Will we see you later, for dinner?" I asked.

"Are you sure?" she asked. "You're already so busy." "Absolutely," I said. "I made chowder, so there's plenty."

"Thanks," she said with a smile. "Besides, if your sister's here, the entertainment alone will be priceless." "I'm hoping you're wrong," I said.

"Me too," she said, with a mischievous grin as she tucked her mug into the dishwasher and grabbed her coat. "Sort of."

∽

By the time I got to the town dock to greet the last mailboat--and hopefully my sister and all the other guests scheduled to arrive--the snow had started to fly. The ground was already white from a storm that had come through the previous week, and there was a fresh dusting on the plowed roads. I said a small prayer for the local lobstermen who were probably still out on the open water--the lobster season in Maine extended to the end of December, and many islanders were still out pulling traps in the sub-zero weather--and then added a small prayer of thanks for my mostly indoor profession.

The wind tore at my coat as I hurried from the van to the dock, passing the local stores that lined it. Although Spurrell's Lobster Pound was closed for winter, Berta Simmons's sea glass jewelry store and Island Artists both kept limited hours as the holiday approached, and the windows twinkled with Christmas lights. I was pleased to see John's boats displayed prominently in the window of the Island Artists store, along with some ornaments he'd designed in the fall; the owner, Selene MacGregor, had told him they were selling well. Once the holiday season was over, I was hoping my husband could turn his attention back to the driftwood sculptures that were starting to take off in some of the galleries on the mainland.

I huddled in the lee of the building, watching for the mail boat. After a few minutes, I heard the thrum of the engine, and watched as the boat churned through the thick, wind-whipped water. As the boat approached the dock, I recognized my sister, who was bundled in a fashion- able puffy jacket, and her husband, Glen, among the small group of passengers. I was just about to head down the gangway when I heard Gwen behind me.

"Aunt Nat!" she called. I turned to see my niece hurrying over to me, her curly dark hair flying in the wind.

"Gwen!" I said. "Where's Adam?"

"He's out pulling up the last of his traps," she told me. Her cheeks were flushed.

"But the wedding's in two days... and aren't his parents coming in?"

Gwen shrugged, but I could tell she was nervous. "He told me he'll be back in a few hours. I just hope the storm holds off."

I glanced up at the darkening sky, then at the whitecaps foaming on the dark water. It decidedly wasn't holding off, but I didn't want to upset Gwen anymore. Adam had been lobstering for years, and was careful, but bad weather wasn't something to mess with.

"Look," she said. "Here they are."

We hurried down the gangway together as the captain leapt lightly off the mailboat and tied her up, then pulled out the plastic steps while his first mate stood by to help his passengers off the pitching boat.

Bridget was first, and pulled first Gwen, and then me, into an expensive-smelling embrace. I pulled away, still smelling spring flowers despite the cold, and then gave my brother-in-law Glen a quick hug.

"We met your future in-laws on the boat," Bridget said. "This is Margaret and James," she said, as an older couple stepped off the boat and onto the dock.

"You must be Gwen," said Margaret, fixing my niece with a penetrating look that reminded me of my sister's. I could sense Gwen shrinking under her future mother-in-law's gaze, and felt a little sorry for her; neither her mother or mother-in-law-to-be seemed like the warm, comforting type.

"Great to meet you," James said, enfolding his future daughter-in-law in a stiff hug. "We've heard so much about you."

"Natalie? Is that you?"

I turned to see what I guessed from the voice must be a man; it was hard to tell with the layers of jacket, scarf, and hat. I surmised it must be my cousin, although he'd been a lot shorter the last time I saw him. "Robert?"

"It's me," he said, flashing me a grin from the depths of his scarf. I gave him a hug. "I haven't seen you in what... twenty years? Thanks so much for making it out. I can't wait to catch up!"

"Can we do it somewhere else?" my sister whined.

"Of course. We should get into the van where it's

warm," I said as the wind gusted. I waved to the captain as he untied the mail boat. As the engine roared back to life, I led everyone back up to the pier toward the van, excited for the chance to catch up with my cousin and hoping things would go well. Gwen was pointing out John's toy boats and his newest experiment, small wooden cars, to her mother when the door to Island Artists popped open and Selene MacGregor emerged, eyes wild behind her sparkly reading glasses.

"Natalie, I'm so glad you're here. Someone robbed the store!"

∼

My plans to catch up with Bridget and escort Adam and Gwen's families were put on hold as Selene dragged me into Island Artists. I loved the colorful, cozy little store, which featured John's work prominently, along with several other local artists. Sea glass mobiles dangled in the frosted windows, locally made stockings and mittens in a rainbow of colors lined the front of the counter, and shelves of beautiful hand-thrown mugs and bowls lined the back wall; I'd had my eye on a beautiful blue pitcher that would be perfect for serving maple syrup for a couple of weeks now.

"See?" she said, pointing to a pile of empty boxes behind the counter. There was a strong smell of gasoline in the place, and a touch of herring; I assumed it was a result of the lobster co-op being located right next door.

"What's missing?" I asked.

"All the toys I was going to donate to the fundraiser," she said, fiddling with the hem of her hand-knitted sweater. My friend Claudette had set up a Christmas fundraiser to help support Marge O'Leary as she recovered from her broken foot; all the local businesses had donated something to be auctioned off. I'd contributed a weekend at the inn, myself. "Someone stole them. I can't believe someone would do a thing like that!"

"When did it happen?" I asked.

"I don't know," she said. "They were here this morning; I finished packing the boxes first thing. I was going to take them over to the church on my way home." She sighed. "Will you ask John to come in and do a report, or whatever it is you do when there's a theft?"

"Of course," I said. Like most islanders, my husband held a variety of jobs. In addition to supplying Island Artists with a good portion of their merchandise, sculpting artwork in his studio, and operating as my partner at the inn, John also served as the island deputy. Things had been quiet since the summer people left; there had been a few (not out of the ordinary) complaints about Claudette White's goats rampaging through local pumpkin patches in October, and one missing poultry case (the hen in question, Niblet, was later found helping herself to the lower branches one of the local apple trees), but other than that, things had been pretty quiet. "I'm sorry this happened; you were generous to give so much to the fundraiser. Were you here all day?"

"I went home to see Fozzie Bear and grab lunch at around one, but other than that, I haven't gone anywhere." Fozzie Bear was Selene's adorable corgi; he sometimes came to the shop to keep her company.

"Did you lock the door?" I asked.

"I think so," she said, fidgeting with her bracelets.

"You think so?"

"I don't know," she said. "I got a call from my daughter just as I was leaving. I think I did... but I just don't remember. But why take the gifts I was going to donate and leave everything else?"

"That's a good question," I said. "What all did you put aside?"

"Three or four of John's boats, a few of these handmade dolls and some doll clothes"--she pointed to a basket of adorable dolls on the counter--"some puzzles, two of the cars John's experimenting with this year, and some wooden tops."

"That's a nice donation," I said.

"It would have been, anyway," she said, still fiddling with her bracelets. "But now it's all gone."

"Where was the box?"

"Right here," she said. As I followed her to the counter, the smell of gasoline and herring grew stronger. I wrinkled my nose, but Selene didn't seem to notice. "Behind the counter. I tucked it in under the register. And now the whole box is gone."

"And you're sure you didn't deliver it?"

"Positive," she said. "I was going to drop it off tonight."

I sighed. "I'm so sorry your donation disappeared. I'll tell John as soon as I get home; there's a storm coming, but I'm sure he'll be out as soon as he can."

"I hate to be a bother, what with the wedding and the holiday coming up, but I really did want to donate to the fundraiser."

"It's a wonderful thing to do," I said, "and I'm so sorry this happened. I'll let John know when I get back to the inn."

"Thanks, Natalie," she said, looking relieved. I wasn't sure what John was going to be able to do about it, but I smiled at her and headed back into the frigid afternoon, hoping everyone at the inn was getting along. After all, they'd only been together for a half hour.

What could go wrong?

~

Evidently, a lot.

My sister met me at the kitchen door, and I hadn't even closed it before she started in. Glen was nowhere to be seen; doubtless he'd run for cover. "Those people are the most insufferable snobs!" she said. "They made some comment about Gwen's degree... as if she weren't 'good enough' for their Princeton-educated son." I closed both the door and my mouth; I didn't feel it would be helpful to point out that she'd felt a mere lobsterman was below her own daughter.

"I'm sure it was nothing," I said. "Is John here?"

"I haven't seen him," she said. "What did that woman at the store need you for? Robbery? I thought this island was safe!"

"Just something that went astray," I said, giving my cats Biscuit and Smudge, who had finally befriended each other and were curled up in front of the heater, a quick hello. "Nothing huge. I'm sure it'll be worked out soon. Where is everyone, anyway?"

"In the parlor," she said.

"I'll get some cookies and hot chocolate out, then," I said. "Can you grab me one of those platters?"

Bridget grabbed the top platter from the stack without breaking stride, continuing to talk as I set to work laying out jam thumbprints, gingerbread cookies and lemon bars. "Now that I think of it," she said, "I still have reservations about this. I mean, this island is idyllic and all, but it's-- pardon me for saying so--a real backwater. I know she's in love, but is she going to regret her decision a few years down the line, when it's too late?"

"I don't think anyone knows for sure how it's going to turn out when they get married," I pointed out as I busied myself pouring milk into a kettle on the stove.

"But really. She'd have so many more opportunities if she'd gone on to get her master's degree. And in California..."

I stifled a sigh. All the progress we seemed to have made the last time my sister visited appeared to have evaporated in the California sun. I'd hoped she was finally on board with Adam and Gwen's decision, but that no longer seemed to be the case. "Why don't you keep an eye on this pot for me?" I asked. "The recipe's right here, and I've got the chocolate and milk powder measured out; there's the corn starch. I'm going down to talk to John."

"But..."

"I'll be right back," I promised, and grabbed my coat and boots. I'd rarely been happier to step out into sub-zero temperatures and a stiff winter wind.

John was finishing work on a last batch of toy cars when I knocked and walked into his sawdust-scented workshop, which was one of the small outbuildings behind the inn. His mother Catherine lived in the other, but I knew today she was visiting with her boyfriend, Murray Selfridge. "I don't want to interfere with the meeting of the families," she had told me as she arranged her pearls and put on her wool winter coat late that morning. She and Charlene were tied for "most stylish islander." Not that there was much competition on Cranberry Island. "I'll come by tomorrow, when things have settled out."

"Thanks for the support," I said wryly.

"Liquor is always helpful," she'd suggested with a grin before nipping out the door.

Now, as I stepped into John's workshop, I found myself wondering if perhaps there might be some merit in the idea. Would anyone notice if I spiked the hot chocolate with bourbon?

Or maybe just served bourbon? "Everyone make it in?" John asked.

"They did," I said. "And Gwen's mom and Adam's mom seem to have a few things in common."

"Oh, that's great!" he said, rubbing a bit of sandpaper over a recently completed toy car. He was dressed in jeans and a green fisherman's sweater that brought out the color of his eyes. His sandy hair was flecked with sawdust, as were the shoulders of his sweater. Not for the first time, I reflected that I was a very lucky woman. He smiled at me. "At least they're getting along, right?"

"I said they had things in common," I replied. "I did not say that they were getting along."

He cocked an eyebrow. "Uh oh. What happened?"

"Apparently Adam's mom made some comment about Gwen not finishing school, and Bridget took it to mean that they don't think her daughter is good enough for their son. So now she's back on the whole 'will she really want to be married to a lobstermen and trapped in this backwater in five years' thing."

John groaned. "She didn't say this in front of Gwen, did she?"

"Not that I know of," I said. "I'm making hot chocolate before braving the parlor. I'm thinking of spiking it."

"Good call."

"It was your mother's idea. But that's not why I'm here..."

"You just missed my company, didn't you?" he asked, eyes sparkling. "Or you're nosy about your Christmas gift."

"Well, yes on both counts," I admitted. "But Selene down at Island Artists told me someone stole all of the toys she'd put aside for the fundraiser."

His expression turned serious. "What? When?"

"Sometime today," I said. "There's nothing else missing, though... at least nothing she's noticed so far."

"That's the third theft this week," he told me. "All related to the Christmas fundraiser."

"Really?" And here I was thinking things had been quiet.

"We've been so busy getting ready for the wedding, I guess I forgot to tell you. Emmeline said someone took the box of candles and scarves she was donating off the front porch yesterday, and another package from one of the shops in Bar Harbor disappeared off the mail boat the day before that."

"Weird!" I said. "Why would someone steal toys going to a fundraiser? I mean, it's a small island; someone's going to notice if their neighbor suddenly turns up with two of your handmade cars under the Christmas tree."

"I'd notice, for sure. I know exactly which ones they are."

"Who would do something like that?"

"Someone desperate to have toys for their own kid for Christmas?" he asked.

"Why not steal one or two from the shelves in the store, where they'd be less easily noticed?" I asked.

He shrugged. "Maybe whoever it is figured she'd think she'd already dropped the box off... or someone had picked it up."

"I'll have to talk to Claudette," I said. Claudette White, owner of the island's renegade goats, was organizing the fundraising sale. The willingness to help neighbors out was one of the things I loved about living on Cranberry Island. It troubled me that someone was interfering with the effort.

He sighed. "I'd talk with Marge, but I don't want to upset her."

"I get it," I said. "In the meantime, we've got enough stuff to deal with at the inn."

"Problems with the wedding plan?"

"Problems with the parents of the bride and groom, I suspect. Like I said, I think both sets think their offspring could have done better."

"Lovely," John said. "Good thing they live far away, then."

"We still have to make it through the next few days; and I don't want them spoiling Gwen and Adam's wedding."

He sighed. "I'm just about done here; why don't I come up and join you?"

"That would be great," I said.

"Then let's go!"

∼

The snow was falling fast and hard; it had already covered the walkway in a light blanket as John closed the workshop door behind him and we hurried back up to the inn. The windows glowed warmly in the cold night; after years of green Christmases in Texas, I was still enjoying the snowy holiday season... even if it did involve a bit more snow-blowing and shoveling than I would have liked. There would be plenty of both in our immediate future, I knew.

We stamped our boots off before stepping into the kitchen. Charlene had reappeared and was sitting at the kitchen table as Bridget stirred the milk on the stove.

"Bridget!" John walked over and gave her a big

hug, and she smiled for the first time since I'd seen her. "So good to see you!" he continued. "Let's go join the others in the parlor; I haven't met everyone yet."

We watched as Bridget allowed John to maneuver her out the kitchen door, and then I heaved a sigh of relief.

"Sounds like things are off to a rocky start," Charlene said.

"Nothing a little Christmas cheer can't help, I hope," I said as I stirred the pot on the stove. "I just hope everyone behaves for the sake of Adam and Gwen."

"I hope so, too," Charlene said.

I stole a glance at my friend. "John tells me there have been some thefts around the island lately."

"Yeah. The fundraiser for Marge."

"You didn't tell me?"

"Sorry," she said. "I figured John knew."

"Any idea what's going on?"

"I know there are a few families down on their luck this year," she said. "Terri Bischoff's catch has been way down; she's thinking they might have to move off-island. And Anna lives on her pension and was making noise about the fundraiser just the other day."

"You told me she had a thing for Frank Duggin. Do you think she's just jealous?"

"That's my guess. Frank offered to have Marge come live with him to cut costs last week. He is completely head-over- heels for her; I think he was hoping her financial situation would work to his advantage."

"That's never a good foundation for a relationship," I said.

"I know. Marge did the right thing and said no, but Anna got wind of it, and boy, was she angry. She came in for coffee, Metamucil, and a pack of Kit Kat bars yesterday, and was complaining about Marge--loudly--to anyone who would listen. Lazy, bad-tempered... you name it, she said it."

"I guess I thought that about Marge too once," I said. Marge had gone through a rough patch several years ago, when she was married to an abusive husband. "But I know better now. Still... do you think she's bitter enough to scuttle the fundraiser?"

"Somebody's messing with it," Charlene said with a shrug, then walked over and took a deep whiff of the contents of the pot. "What magic are you making?"

"Hot chocolate," I said.

"This isn't the kind I make out of a package," she said.

"No," I agreed. "It may involve some bourbon. Social

lubricant and all."

"Either that or it'll be like throwing gasoline on a fire," she pointed out. "We'll find out, right? Who all is here, anyway?"

"Bridget and her husband Glen. And Adam's parents, Margaret and James. My cousin Robert is in town, too."

"You mentioned him," she said. "He moved to Bangor recently, right?"

"He did," I confirmed. Gwen's in there holding court, with John to back her up; Adam should be here any moment."

"Small group," my friend observed.

"Adam and Gwen are both only children," I said. "Besides, Gwen wanted to keep it intimate."

"Only children, eh? No wonder their parents think no one's good enough," Charlene said with a grimace.

As she spoke, headlights appeared at the top of the drive. "I'll bet that's Adam," I said.

"Does he know what he's walking into?" Charlene asked.

"We'll find out soon enough!" I said cheerily and tasted the hot chocolate. "Oh, that's good," I said. I gave it another stir, added some bourbon, then poured the chocolate into a big pitcher and put it on a tray with some mugs, then retrieved the vanilla whipped cream I'd made earlier from the fridge. I'd just added another splash of bourbon when Adam appeared at the kitchen door.

"Perfect timing," I told him. "We were just about to have hot chocolate and cookies."

"Did everyone make it here?" he asked, stamping the snow off his boots one last time and unwinding a red-and- white-striped scarf from around his neck.

"They did," I said, not wanting to spook him by letting him know they appeared to be drawing the battle lines already. As he took off his jacket, revealing a fisherman's sweater much like John's, only in oatmeal, I turned to my friend, who was adding a few more gingerbread men to the tray of cookies I'd laid out. "Charlene, will you grab the cookies? We'll all go in together."

"Strength in numbers," she murmured, and Adam held the swinging door for us as we filed out of the kitchen and into the dining room. I could already hear animated voices from the parlor beyond.

"Adam majored in business," Margaret was announcing as I walked in. "His professor wanted him to submit some of his work to the *New Yorker*."

"Gwen majored in art," Bridget riposted. "She's so talent- ed... she got a full scholarship for her work last year..."

"Hot chocolate and cookies, anyone?" I asked, interrupting my sister.

"Those look amazing," Gwen said. Adam was beside her; I noticed they were holding hands so tightly their knuckles were white.

"I added a bit of bourbon for an extra warm-up. Who's up for a 'special' hot chocolate?"

"Me!" Adam and Gwen responded in unison. "You should try it, Mom," Gwen said.

"So, should you," Adam said, directing the comment at his own mother.

"I really shouldn't..."

"It's the holiday season," I said. "Everyone in?"

When the assembled party nodded, I set down the tray and got to work. "This is my best friend Charlene," I said as I poured a healthy slug into each mug.

"Good to meet you," Adam's father said, standing up as Charlene extended a hand; a moment later, his wife, Margaret, introduced herself. Bridget already knew her, of course, but my brother-in-law hadn't met her yet. Nor, I realized, had my cousin, who was staring at Charlene and looked a bit as if he'd been knocked between the eyes with a two-by-four.

"This is my cousin Robert," I supplied for him, since he seemed incapable of speech. "I told you about him, Charlene; he just moved to Bangor a few months ago."

"So good to meet you," she said.

"Please... sit down," he said, gesturing to an empty spot on the sofa next to him.

"Thanks," she said, blushing and reaching up to adjust her hair. I bit back a smile as I poured the last of the hot chocolate into the mugs and then added a dollop of whipped cream to each. As I passed the mugs out, Charlene and Robert hardly noticed me; they were deep in conversation, completely oblivious to the plate of cookies or to the continuing sparring going on between the two sets of parents. Instead of focusing on their children, they were both trying to prove the superiority of their respective offspring. I glanced out the window, where the snow was already starting to accumulate. I had a wedding to prepare for, and it looked like I was going to spend the next 48 hours trying to keep Gwen and Adam's mothers from challenging each other to a duel.

"So," Bridget said. "What was Adam's major?"

"Business," Margaret said proudly. "He's not using it at the moment, but he could. I guess Gwen just decided to launch out on her own before finishing school, eh?"

Gwen colored, her lips a thin line.

"She finished. It just took her a few extra years," Bridget said, "but she got seduced. I'm not sure if it was your son or this island, but all of our plans kind of got derailed."

That, it seemed, was the final straw. Gwen stood up and glared at both of them. "Look," she said. Adam reached for her hand and squeezed it, looking equally piqued. "I've tried to be polite, but this has got to stop."

"What?" Adam's mother said, blinking.

"This... comparing us like we're prize horses. Adam and I are adults. We've chosen each other. And if this continues..."

A furrow appeared in Bridget's forehead. "Gwen, honey... what?"

"Maybe we shouldn't be getting married this weekend," she said. "Now if you'll excuse me, I've got things to do." She stood up, brushed off her skirt, and marched to the door to the kitchen with a flustered Adam in her wake.

I took a sip of my hot chocolate, which was so thick it was almost custardy, but with a lovely warm kick, and glanced at John. So much for a peaceful holiday season and a magical wedding.

A stunned silence had fallen over the room. Before anyone could break it, the phone rang. I jumped up to answer it, thankful for any excuse to leave the parlor. When I got to the kitchen, there was no sign of Gwen or Adam; I was guessing they'd gone upstairs to Gwen's room to talk.

"Good evening, Gray Whale Inn," I said as I picked up the phone, my eye on the staircase.

"Natalie, is that you?" It was my good friend Eleazer White. He and his wife, Claudette, were islanders through and through; I was thankful that they'd accepted me as one of their own. Now, though, I could hear distress in his voice.

"Eli? What's wrong?"

"Claudette is just beside herself," he said.

"What? Why? Is she okay?"

"You know all those things she collected and took down to the church for Marge's fundraiser?"

"Yes," I said. I had a bad feeling about this.

"It's all gone," he said.

"What?"

"Every last bit. I was trying to fix Frank Duggin's motor-- he was over here yesterday, and it's still leakin' gasoline all over creation--while Claudie went down to start organizing things into baskets. She just called to say somebody stole them."

I sighed. Who on earth would intentionally torch a fundraiser dedicated to one of the islanders? "I'll send John down," I said. "Where should I tell him to go?"

"Claudette's down at the church."

"Got it," I said, thinking maybe John could use some company. Besides, anything to get me out of range of extended family was a welcome distraction. I had just hung up the phone, wondering what else could go wrong, when the power went out, shrouding the inn in darkness.

∾

"Tough crowd," John said as we hurried out to the van a few minutes later. I'd distributed candles and flashlights; with the exception of Charlene and my cousin, all the other guests had dispersed to their own corners, doubtless to continue their complaining in private. Our heat wasn't electric, thankfully, so the place would be warm, but I hadn't gotten around to picking up a generator yet, so our lighting options were limited. Was the whole island blacked out? I wondered. And would the power come on in time for the wedding?

Assuming there was a wedding, that was.

"It's kind of a relief to be in the van," John said. "Do you think Gwen was serious about calling the wedding off?"

"I don't know," I said. "I don't think she's not

going to marry Adam. It's just whether she's going to do it when her family's here, I think."

"They were pretty poorly behaved," John said.

"You think? I'm disappointed in Bridget; I thought she'd come to terms with things."

"I think Margaret's dissing her daughter has rekindled some of that. I can't say I blame her."

I sighed as John put the van into drive and headed up the rapidly whitening driveway. Fortunately, neither John nor I had had any of the spiked hot chocolate, so we were good to drive. I just hoped the two families didn't burn down the inn while we were gone.

"At least Gwen and Adam have some things in common."

"What do you mean?'

"Two Tiger Moms," I said as we crested the hill on our way to the church; the snow was falling so quickly that the wipers could barely keep up. We couldn't stay at the church long unless we wanted to walk home, I thought. Although it might be preferable to bunk at the church. Certainly less stressful. "No wonder Gwen and Adam both moved to an island only accessible by boat."

John squinted through the snow on the windshield. "Unfortunately, it looks they're probably going to be snowed in with them for a while."

"They can go back to Adam's place," I pointed out. "We're the ones who may be stuck with them."

"Thanks for reminding me," he said glumly. "On the plus side," he said, brightening a bit, "Charlene and Robert seemed to hit it off."

"That's true," I said as we pulled into the church parking lot next to Claudette's beaten-up station wagon. The church was dark, as was the rest of the island; the power outage must have covered the whole community. The headlights illuminated the little church; the snow on the roof and the pine trees made it look like something from a Currier and Ives painting. "I wish I knew Robert better. We haven't seen each other in twenty years."

"If they do get along, at least he's in Bangor, not Port- land," John pointed out.

"Let's not put the cart before the horse," I suggested. "She's just recovering from the last break up, and I have no idea what kind of man Robert turned into, although he was very nice as a boy."

"True," he said. "I guess I'm just a romantic."

"A romantic deputy," I said, and reached over to squeeze his gloved hand. "Speaking of deputing, what do you think is going on with these fundraiser thefts?" I asked.

"Either someone's desperate for money, or someone doesn't like Marge, is my guess."

"Who are you thinking?" I asked.

"Well, Marge took a few jobs from Bertha Matheson this past summer, I hear," John said. "So Bertha's one possibility." "Huh. Charlene told me Frank Duggin has a crush on Marge, too," I said.

John blinked. "Really Frank?"

"He writes her poetry. Brings her flowers."

"Hidden depths, that one. I've heard him wax rhapsodic over an upgraded motor, but I thought his lady love was his lobster boat."

"Apparently his lady love has had some mechanical issues lately, leaving him stranded at the store. That's when he fell for Marge."

"Really."

"Really. And what's more, it's a love triangle."

John stared at me, openmouthed. "No."

"Yes. Charlene told me Anna is livid with Marge. She wants Frank for herself."

"She does?" John said, sounding puzzled. "But he smells like a bait shop."

"No accounting for taste," I said. "Maybe she's grown up around that smell so much that she doesn't notice it. And as Charlene has pointed out repeatedly, now that you and Adam are spoken for, the pickings on Cranberry Island are rather slim."

"Maybe," John said, not sounding convinced. "You

think Anna would be vindictive enough to steal a bunch of toys over that?"

I shrugged. "All's fair in love and war, right?"

He sighed. "Well, let's go find out what Claudette has to say."

Together, we hurried from the van to the church door; John held it for me while I nipped inside, along with a flurry of snowflakes, and then followed me.

Our flashlights illuminated the sanctuary of the little church, which was decorated for Christmas with greenery and red ribbons adorning the pews and altar. I took a deep breath, enjoying the scent of pine and furniture polish and candle wax and a little bit of dust; it was familiar and comforting and would have felt deeply satisfying had it not been for Claudette's anxious voice echoing off the walls.

"Natalie? John? Is that you?"

"It's us," I confirmed.

"Thank goodness you're here," she said, appearing with a lantern in hand. Claudette's solid frame was swathed in a chunky wool sweater, a broomstick skirt, and boots. "I just can't believe this is happening."

"When did you discover that things were missing?" John asked.

"Just a half hour ago," she told me. "I came up to sort things out before the storm got worse, and when I opened the door to the bride's room... well, you'll see."

We followed her down the aisle to a door to the right of the altar, and then into the bride's room, a small room that doubled as a dressing room and a storage area.

"Look!" she said, pointing to a long, empty table. "It's all gone."

"All the donations?" John asked.

Claudette nodded, almost in tears. "Every one of them. I've kept the door locked, but when I got here today, it was open."

"When was that?" John asked.

"Just when I called," she said. "They were all here this morning! And I've heard whoever it was stole things from a few other places, too." Her shoulders sagged. "I just can't believe it. We're all supposed to be working together here!"

"Maybe it was someone in need?" I suggested.

"Whoever it was sloppy," John said, squatting down and looking at the table. "There's something like grease on the side of the table. Was this here before?"

"No," Claudette said, peering at the smear of what looked like dirty engine grease.

"There are footprints, too," I said, pointing at the

wood floor. "Or what used to be, before the snow melted."

"It was recent, then," John said. "The water hasn't evaporated."

"Not much of a clue, though. No footprints, really. Just melted snow."

"Could be anyone," Claudette said glumly.

"We'll do our best to figure it out," John said semi-comfortingly. "And if not, never fear; we'll take care of Marge."

"It just isn't neighborly," she said. "I don't understand it." "We'll take care of it," I said soothingly, glancing at

John and hoping we weren't making promises we couldn't keep.

∽

"So, who do you think it was?" I asked John as we hurried back to the van a few minutes later.

"I don't know," he said. "I'd say someone who's hit hard times, but what are they going to do with a bunch of toys?"

"It's almost like someone has it in for Marge," I said. "Maybe it's Anna."

"You suggested that before. You really think she'd try to kill the fundraiser because she's jealous?"

"Hell hath no fury like a woman scorned," I said. "Maybe we should stop by and visit?"

"We'd better do it before the snow gets too bad," he said. "She lives up on Seal Point Road, doesn't she?"

"She does," I confirmed, and a few minutes later, we pulled up outside a tiny two-story house. Candlelight flick- ered in the windows, and snow was already starting to drift across the small porch.

"At least she's home," John said. As we got out of the van, John walked over to the beaten-up golf cart in the driveway. There were no tracks; it didn't appear to have moved all day. Nor, I confirmed with a sweep of the flashlight, were there any tracks off the front porch or along the sides of the house."

Anna answered the door almost immediately. She was a small, neat-looking woman with tortoise-shell glasses; tonight, she was bundled up in a jacket and mittens. "Can I help you?" she asked.

"John and Natalie from the Gray Whale Inn; I know we've met a few times before," John said. "Can we come in for a minute?"

"Of course," she said. "It's a bit chilly in here; the wind keeps shooting down the chimney and filling the place with smoke. I keep meaning to get that looked at," she said as she closed the door behind us. "Come and sit down, please," she said, leading us to a plaid couch in her small living room. "Can I get you anything?"

"No thanks," I said.

"Likewise," John said. "As for your fireplace, 'll take a look when the weather clears," he offered. "But in the meantime... can I ask you a few questions?"

She perched on the rocking chair by the fire. "What kind of questions?"

"Where were you this evening?" John asked.

"Here," she told him steadily.

"The whole time?"

She nodded. "I haven't left the place since yesterday. I'm just snuggling in with my kitties." She pointed to the two orange tabbies curled up on a cushion by the fire.

John got up, walked over to the back door, and shone his light out at the ground, then turned back to Anna. "Do you have any idea who might want to interfere with the fundraiser for Marge O'Leary?" he asked.

Her face tightened. "No," she said shortly, then, "Why?"

"Someone stole all of the donations," I said. "We're trying to find out who did it."

"So you must know she isn't my favorite person, if you're here asking me questions," she said.

"We've heard," John admitted.

"I asked him to dinner last month," she admitted. "He declined. And now he's chasing down Marge O'Leary. Marge! She treats him horribly." She swiped at her eyes and took a deep breath. "But no, to answer your question. Other than me, I don't know who would have it in for Marge."

"I'm so sorry," I said. "That's got to be rough."

"One of the downsides of living on an island," John said. "I've been there, too."

"Have you?" she asked, looking slightly hopeful.

"I have," he confirmed.

She sighed. "At least I have my kitties. They don't ask for much, and they don't make a terrible mess." She looked up at me. "I keep telling myself it's for the best. I'd spend all my time trying to get him to tidy up. I don't quite know what I see in him, frankly."

I didn't either, but I decided to keep that to myself.

"Are you sure you won't have any tea?" she asked.

"We'd love to," John said, "but we'd better get back before the snow gets too deep." He glanced at the fireplace, which appeared to be the small house's only source of heat. "Do you have enough wood?"

"I've got plenty on the back porch," she said. "I've seen worse winters than this; you don't need to worry about me."

"Well, if you run into trouble, give us a call," I said. "We've got plenty of rooms."

"Thanks," she said as we got up and walked to the door. "I'm sorry I wasn't more help."

"It's just fine," John said. "Stay warm!" he said, and a moment later, we were back out in the cold night and no closer to figuring out what had happened to all those toys.

∽

Gwen was waiting for us at the kitchen table when we got home, looking morose in the light of a single candle.

"Where's Adam?" I asked.

"He went home," she said. "I told him I needed time to think."

"About what?" I asked, pulling up a chair across the table from her as John busied himself making a pot of decaf; we were both still chilled.

She gave me a look.

"Are you having second thoughts about the wedding?" I asked.

She sighed. "I am."

"Really?"

"I just want it to be about us. Not about everybody's idea of what we should be, or what we should have done with our lives."

"I get it," I said.

"I want to marry Adam... he's the love of my life. But I don't want the whole thing spoiled by our parents. I'd rather just elope."

"You can elope here if you want," I said. "I could call the priest and we could head over anytime. As long as you don't mind a very small, candlelight service."

"You'd do that for me?"

"Of course," I said. "We can have a reception or not, it's up to you. This is about you and Adam. Nobody else matters."

She reached across the table and squeezed my hand. "Thanks, Aunt Nat," she said. She bit her lip, and I could see the uncertainty her mother always managed to spark in her. "You don't think I'm crazy for building my life here, do you?"

As she spoke, John came up behind me and rested his hands on my shoulders. A wave of love and gratitude filled me, and I grinned at my niece. "I can only speak for myself, but I'm happier here than I have been anywhere else in my entire life."

Gwen's shoulders sagged, and her face relaxed a little bit. "Thanks. It's just... I'm fine when it's just

Adam and me, but then these other people come in, and I feel like I'm defending myself all the time."

"I know," I said. After all, I'd grown up with Bridget. "I'm sorry it's so hard, but it's only temporary. As for the wedding... you'll think about it?"

"I'll think about it," she said, then turned to John. "Got enough coffee for three?"

"Of course," he said, and we spent a companionable hour by candlelight, enjoying the warmth of family. With only a slight shadow cast by judgy relatives... and an unsolved crime.

∽

It was the night before the maybe-wedding, and I was busy in the kitchen, baking cake tiers and mini quiches for the post-wedding celebration. Assuming Gwen and Adam decided to go through with it; she'd been mum on the topic after we talked. We were still snowed in, but I'd borrowed a generator from Eleazer so that I could get the cooking done, and Tom Lockhart had promised he'd find a way to clear the road to the church. Not for the first time, I felt myself lucky to live in such a close community.

"I really think Princeton is the best of the Ivy League," Margaret was droning on as I nipped into the dining room to grab a pitcher from the sideboard. There was no sign and Adam or Gwen; it was just the two sets of parents, continuing to joust.

"Is there more wine, Nat?" Bridget asked, her face already flushed.

"Come with me, and I'll get you some," I said. She excused herself and followed me into the kitchen.

"Have you seen Gwen at all?" my sister asked.

"Not recently," I said, "but you guys have got to tone it down."

Bridget blinked. "Tone it down? I'm not the one going on about the Ivy League every thirty seconds."

"You can't control what other people do, but you can control what you do," I said. "This is about Gwen and Adam. Not about anything else."

"I know," she said peevishly. "I just want what's best for her."

"I understand," I said as I handed her a bottle from the pantry. "But I don't think it's working in your favor."

Her lips were a thin line. "I don't want her marrying some smelly lobsterman."

"Adam is not smelly," I said. "They work with bait and engines, but they do understand basic hygiene. Wait..."

"What?"

"I've got to talk to John," I said. "Corkscrew's in

the dining room. Help yourself," I said, and left her standing there.

John was busy in his workshop when I burst through the door a few minutes later.

"What's going on?" he asked, looking up from a tangle of driftwood he was planning to turn into a mermaid.

"I'll tell you on the way," I said.

∼

We might not have power yet, but fortunately, Tom had gotten enough of the roads plowed that we didn't have to wade through snow to get to our destination. Within fifteen minutes, we pulled up outside a small mobile home not far from the lobster co-op, parking next to a beaten-up truck. A stack of lobster traps covered with snow stood a few yards away from the small building.

John made a face as we got out of the van. Even with the cold, I could smell the distinctive aroma of bait and gasoline and wrinkled my nose.

"Right there," I said, pointing to a set of snowed-over footprints leading from the truck toward a ramshackle shed on the edge of the woods. Together, we followed the tracks. There was no padlock on the door, and it was slightly ajar.

"It's open. Shall we take a quick peek?" I asked John, who always gave me a hard time for snooping. "Or is that being too nosy?"

"Well, since it's open..." John pulled the flashlight he kept in his pocket out, aimed it at the crack in the door, then sighed.

"What do you see?"

"Look for yourself," he said, stepping aside so I could peek in.

A jumble of colorful toys filled a box lightly dusted with snow; I could make out one of John's boats among the toys, along with a few of the dolls from Island Artists and some books.

"What I don't understand is, why?" John asked. "If he likes Marge, why would he try to make things difficult for her?"

"He's in love with her," I explained. "He wants to be her knight in shining armor. My guess is that he was hoping she'd be desperate enough to agree to move in with him, or at least accept help from him."

As I spoke, there was the sound of a door opening some- where behind me.

"Who's there?"

We turned to see Frank's round figure in the doorway to the mobile home. "John Quinton, your friendly local deputy," John said. "I'd like to talk with you, if you have a minute."

There was a brief silence, and then, "It's not what you think."

"I hope not," John said. "But I'm struggling to come up with an alternate explanation."

∽

"It was a stupid idea," Frank said. He'd offered us both beers--we'd declined--and was ensconced in a La-Z-Boy that had seen better days, while John and I perched on a battered couch across from him. The place was littered with old newspapers, beer cans, and dirty plates, and Frank's distinctive fish/gasoline aroma was thick in the air; I could see why Marge wasn't keen on moving in. "When she turned me down to go steady, I... I didn't know what to do."

"So you tried to gut the fundraiser so you could sweep in to the rescue and she'd feel like she had to say yes," I guessed.

He nodded, and the blood rushed to his face. "It was a stupid plan, I know."

"Not the best basis for a relationship, I'll say that," I said.

"I know, I know," he said. "But I don't know what else to do."

"Have you asked her out?" John asked.

"I asked her over for Spam loaf a few weeks

back." He shrugged. "She came, but she only stayed for a few minutes; she barely touched it."

Spam loaf? John and I exchanged glances.

"I know, it's not fancy. I'm not much of a cook, I guess, and money's been tight."

"Got it," John said. "Did you clean the place up at all?"

"A bit," he said. "Put the toilet paper on the roll and got rid of the empties. Even cleared part of the table," he said, nodding toward a small Formica table covered in a jumble of debris.

"Well, that's something," I said.

"It's just... lonely this time of year, I guess. I was hoping Marge would want to share it with me." He looked to John. "You found yourself a wife. Any advice?"

"Natalie might be more helpful than me," he said, "but my first instinct is that you might want to start with a shower and some serious tidying."

"But love should be about what's on the inside," he complained.

"She's not going to find out what's on the inside unless she can get close to the outside comfortably," John pointed out. "But before we get into house cleaning, you need to return the things you stole. And hope nobody presses charges."

He paled. "Charges?"

"Charges," John repeated. "Written apologies might help."

"But then Marge will know what I did!"

"It's Cranberry Island," John pointed out. "It's not like you're going to be able to keep things under wraps."

"Besides," I said, "maybe she'll think it's romantic." Although desperate and creepy were closer to the mark.

"You think?" he asked, brightening. He was a good person, even though he was a little clueless.

"We'll find out," John said. "Now let's get this stuff loaded up. I don't know if we can get to the church today, but I can take it tomorrow if I need to."

He let out a heavy sigh and stood up. "I suppose you're right," he said. "What's Marge going to say?"

"If I were you, I'd get in touch with her before she hears it through the grapevine."

His doughy face was as white as the snow. "Will I go to jail?"

"I can't make any promises about that, but if I were you, I'd start working on those apologies today," John advised. "Now, let's get that shed unlocked and load up the van."

∽

While we'd been off solving one problem, alas, another one seemed to have boiled over.

We could hear the sound of raised voices even before we got to the inn. "Uh oh," I said as John and I stamped the snow off our boots and headed back into the inn, feeling dread.

When we walked into the parlor, with the exception of Adam and Gwen, the two families had retreated to their respective sides of the room and the tension was thicker than frozen fudge. Even the cats had retreated from the fire- place and gone into hiding.

"We're just talking!" Margaret protested.

"No," Adam corrected her. "You've been pitting us against each other since you arrived, measuring us against one another. And it stops now."

"I really don't know what you're talking about," James said, drawing himself up.

"Yes, you do," Adam corrected him. He reached for Gwen and put an arm around her. "This is my bride. The love of my life. If you can't treat her with respect, you will not be attending the ceremony."

Adam's mother blanched, and a small, catlike smile had crept over Bridget's face.

Until Gwen turned to her parents and announced, "The same goes for you. Both of you. All of you. We invited you to share our joy, not harpoon it."

"But..." Bridget started.

"No, Mom," Gwen said. "No buts. Adam's going home now, and I'm going upstairs. You can make your cases in the morning. Good night."

And with that, the couple marched out of the parlor, leaving four parents dumbfounded.

I wanted to burst into applause but thought better of it.

∽

"So, what do you think they'll do?" John asked as we got ready for bed. The cats were snuggled into the comforter already; it was chilly in the inn, and they were staying far away from the warring factions downstairs.

"I don't know," I said. "The wedding's on, at least. Gwen told me she and Adam are going through with it--Charlene's doing her hair and make-up in the morning--but she and Adam will decide tomorrow whether their parents are invited."

"They should be able to swallow their pride and act decently for one day, don't you think?"

"I hope so," I said. "But either way, I love that Adam and Gwen stuck up for each other. It bodes well."

"It does," he agreed, and together we snuggled down under the comforter, both wondering what the morning would bring.

∼

The day of the wedding dawned clear and bright... and, thankfully, with power, I discovered when the lights all blinked on at four in the morning. The snow had stopped falling during the night, and the wind had died down, leaving Cranberry Island looking like something out of a Christmas card. Snow blanketed the slopes leading down from the inn to the dark blue water, the pines were frosted white, and the cerulean sky was cloudless.

I headed downstairs to make coffee before everyone got up, only to find Gwen at the kitchen table, cradling a mug.

"You're up early," I said. "Wedding jitters?"

"No," she said, smiling. Her lovely face was glowing. "I made a big pot of coffee and put out some muffins," she said, gesturing toward the counter. "I had a talk with Mom a little while ago, and Adam talked with his parents. I think it'll go on as planned."

"Really?" I asked, doubtfully.

"Really," she said quietly. "I know she wants something different for me. But it's my life. I love her, but I'm not going to give up Adam, my art, you and John, and my life here on the island just to chase a dream that isn't even mine."

"And she understood that?"

Gwen nodded. "She did... and she apologized."

"Really?"

"She did. I think she just wants to be sure she's doing right by me. When really, it's about me doing right by me."

I smiled at my wise niece. "Adam's a lucky man, you know."

"And I'm a lucky woman," she said. "Thanks so much for inviting me here all those years ago. You've changed my life. For the better."

Which was the best Christmas present anyone could ever have given me.

~

The church was completely full when the first bars of music played, the smell of candle wax and Christmas greenery filling the air. Adam stood at the front of the church, looking like a romance novel hero in his crisp tux, even though I noticed him running a finger around the inside of his collar;

none of us was used to dressing up. A moment later, the whole church turned to see my niece, Gwen, step into the church.

She wore a cream-colored satin sleeveless gown that set off her pale shoulders. Her dark hair was a tumble of curls, as always, and she carried a small nosegay of cream-colored roses interspersed with red berries and a few sprigs of pine. There was an audible intake of breath as she walked down the aisle flanked by her proud parents, eyes shining. Although the dress was beautiful, she'd have been gorgeous in a burlap sack. I glanced back to Adam; his handsome jaw had dropped at the sight of his bride.

I smiled at Gwen, who had eyes only for her future husband, and as she joined him at the altar, I looked back the rest of the folks in the pews. Marge had made it to the ceremony, as had Frank, who had evidently dressed up for the occasion in his best overalls and was actually sitting next to the object of his affection; he might have been the only other person in the church not staring at Gwen, as his eyes were firmly fixed on Marge. Claudette and Eli were toward the front; Claudette seemed to have recovered, although I thought I saw her dart a glare at Frank. A few pews up, Charlene stood next to Robert, smiling, as was my cousin, who seemed enchanted by my friend; I had hopes for that potential connection. But more importantly, Adam's mother Margaret and my sister Bridget, whose own dark, curly hair was swept up in a beautiful updo, were now standing next to each other in the first pew, if not beaming, then at least not frowning. As I watched, Margaret leaned over to whisper something into Bridget's ear, and her face broke into a sunny smile as she nodded and whispered something back.

"It's a Christmas miracle," I murmured to John, who had also seen the exchange. As the priest began the ceremony, I took a deep breath, suddenly overwhelmed by gratitude for all of the good things in my life. As I dabbed a tear from the corner of my eye, John kissed me on the head and reached for my hand.

And together, hands clasped, we watched as two of our favorite people joined their lives together in love.

NATALIE'S EMERGENCY HOT CHOCOLATE

INGREDIENTS

- 2 cups whole milk (3 if you like slightly thinner hot choco- late--this is super thick!)
- 1/2 cup milk powder
- 1 teaspoon cornstarch
- 1 cup bittersweet (60%) chocolate chips or chopped chocolate
- 1.5 - 2 oz. Bourbon, Kahlúa, peppermint schnapps, or other liqueur

DIRECTIONS

In a medium saucepan, bring milk to a boil over medium-high. Lower the heat to medium and add the chocolate, whisking constantly until the chocolate is completely melted. Then whisk in the milk powder and cornstarch until everything is dissolved and the mixture is smooth and thick. Whisk in liqueur if using.

Serves four.

GRAY WHALE INN GINGERBREAD PEOPLE

INGREDIENTS

- 2-3/4 cups all purpose flour
- 2 teaspoons baking soda
- Heaping 1/4 teaspoon salt
- 2 teaspoons ground ginger
- 1 teaspoon ground cinnamon
- 1/2 teaspoon ground allspice
- 1/4 teaspoon ground cloves
- 1/8 teaspoon freshly ground black pepper
- 1-1/2 sticks unsalted butter, softened
- 1/4 cup plus 2 tablespoons granulated sugar
- 1/4 cup plus 2 tablespoons packed dark brown sugar

- 1 large egg
- 6 tablespoons molasses
- Royal icing for decorating

DIRECTIONS

In a medium bowl, whisk together the flour, baking soda, salt, ginger, cinnamon, allspice, cloves, and black pepper. In the bowl of an electric mixer, beat the butter and sugars on medium speed until light and fluffy (about 2 minutes), then beat in the egg and molasses.

Add the flour mixture and mix on low speed until combined, then divide the dough in half and shape into two flat rounds. Wrap the rounds in plastic wrap and chill in the refrigerator until firm, at least 1 hour.

While dough is chilling, preheat the oven to 350° and line two baking sheets with parchment paper. Place two racks near the center of the oven.

Remove the dough from the refrigerator (if the dough has been in the fridge for longer than an hour, let it sit at room temperature for 10 to 15 minutes and knead it briefly before rolling.) Place the dough on a lightly floured work surface and dust the dough lightly with flour. Roll, turning and adding more flour under and over the dough as neces- sary, to about 1/8-inch thick for crisper cookies or 1/4-inch thick for softer cookies. Cut out shapes with a cookie cutter and transfer the cookies to the prepared baking sheets, using a spatula if necessary. Gather the dough scraps and knead into a ball, then roll out and cut again, adding more flour as necessary. Repeat until all scraps are used up.

Bake the cookies, rotating the sheets from top to bottom and front to back midway through, for 8 to 10 minutes or until they feel firm. Let the cookies cool on the baking sheets for several minutes until set, then transfer to a rack. Repeat until all dough is used up.

When the cookies are completely cool, decorate with icing. Let the icing set completely, a few hours, then store in an airtight container.

Royal Icing

Ingredients:

3 egg whites (pasteurized if you have concerns)

4 cups confectioners sugar

Food coloring (optional)

Directions:

Put the egg whites in the bowl of an electric mixer fitted with the whisk attachment or beaters. Beat on medium speed until frothy.

Add the confectioners' sugar and beat on low speed until sugar is blended in. Increase the speed to medium-low and beat until the mixture is thick and shiny, 3 to 5 minutes.

Divide the icing into bowls, use food coloring to tint the icing, and then add water until icing reaches a good consistency. Cover the icing with a damp paper towel to keep a skin from forming on top. For longer storage, cover bowls tightly with plastic wrap and refrigerate.

LUPINE LIES

LUPINE LIES

Some women collect men like a flower collects bees.

I'd never been one of them, but my friend Charlene was as in-demand as the first lupine of the Maine spring season.

As I finished cleaning up after breakfast, she showed up at the kitchen door, laden with grocery bags. Her caramel-colored hair gleamed in the morning light and her mascaraed lashes were long around her blue eyes. I couldn't blame the male residents of the island, really; not only was she a fun person to be with, but she was gorgeous.

"I brought your groceries. Is he here?" she asked in a low voice, eyes darting around as if she expected someone to have hidden himself behind the curtains, or perhaps in one of the cabinets. She was referring to Alex Van der Berg, the wildlife photographer/naturalist she had broken up with a while back, informing him she couldn't have a relationship with someone she saw a grand total of two weeks a year. He hadn't taken the news well, and although Charlene had moved on—this time to a handsome man I approved of completely, my cousin Robert—Alex, evidently had not.

"I think I saw him go out with his camera," I told her as I opened the screen door.

"Whew." She lugged in the bags, plopping them on the counter. I eyed them with interest; I was hoping caramels and a big bag of walnuts might be in them. I had plans to try out a new chocolate salted-caramel walnut cookie bar recipe. "How long is he staying, again?" Charlene asked, distracting me from my thoughts of food.

"His reservation is through Sunday," I told her.

"Five more days," she groaned. "That's a long time."

"Can you go to Bangor and stay with Robert?"

"Not unless you want the store and the post office closed half the week," she said. "He spent two hours sitting at the bar yesterday, begging me to reconsider. And now I'm getting these weird bouquets on my front porch."

"You're just irresistible," I said with a smile.

"Or something. Yesterday it was these weird

alien-looking flowers, and today was a huge bunch of carnations. Two years ago I would have been over the moon, but now I just wish he'd stop."

"I presume you've told him that?"

"Three times," she said, sitting down at my big pine table as I unloaded the bags. The kitchen glowed in the afternoon light, the walls warm and buttery. My two cats, Biscuit and Smudge, lounged in a spot of sunshine on the wood floors, and the air smelled like lemon soap and vanilla. Charlene plopped her elbows down on the table. "He won't listen. Plus, I'm getting these." She slapped an envelope down on the counter; on it was her name and address, in bold, jagged letters.

"What's this?"

"A poisoned pen letter," she said.

"What?" I asked. "From whom?"

"That's the thing about poisoned pen letters," she said. "They don't usually sign them."

"What's it say, if you don't mind my asking?"

She grimaced. "It says I should stay away from men before another one dies," she said, and although her tone was light, I could tell the letter-writer had hit a nerve. "It called me a Black Widow."

"Wow," I said as I located the bag of walnuts and stowed them in the pantry next to the pecans. "What a horrible thing to write."

"But it's true," she said, looking troubled. "The men I've dated... so many have had terrible fates." She hadn't had the best luck in the dating department, it was true. More than one of her beaus had met a nasty end.

"What about Alex?" I asked. "He's alive and well, to say the least."

"Unfortunately," Charlene said, groaning.

"And so's Robert." Charlene started dating my cousin some months ago, and I'd never seen her happier. I was hoping he might pop the question soon, in fact, although I hadn't broached the topic with either of them.

"But both of those are long-distance relationships," she pointed out. "What if it's the amount of time I spend with them? Maybe they're safe only because they live somewhere else."

"Charlene," I said, setting down the caramels I'd pulled from one of the bags and walking over to put my hand on hers. "Whoever wrote this is simply jealous. You are beautiful, and half the men on the island would give their right arm to date you. Everything that happened in the past was just... bad luck." I paused for a moment. "Robert was just down last weekend, wasn't he?"

"He was," she said.

"Anyone on the island seem to be sweet on him?"

"Yes, actually," Charlene said. "Whenever Robert's in town, Fern spends all her time on the couches in the front of the store, waiting to pounce on him."

"And when did the first missive arrive?"

"Yesterday," she said. "I found it taped to the front door."

"May I read it?" I asked.

She shrugged. "Be my guest."

I slid the letter out of the envelope.

"BLACK WIDOW. STAY AWAY FROM MEN BEFORE ANOTHER ONE DIES." The handwriting was jagged, but the 'ws' were oddly curvy, with an unusual flourish.

"I don't recognize the handwriting," I said, "but that sounds like a threat. I think we should show this to John."

"Really?" she asked. I just... it's embarrassing."

"I think whoever wrote this is deeply disturbed," I said. "We need to let him know about this. You didn't see anyone who might have dropped this off?"

"No," she said, shaking her head. "I hate thinking that someone on the island feels that way about me."

"We'll get it figured out," I said, trying to sound reassuring. I finished emptying the bags and sat down across from her. Biscuit looked up at me and mewed, then closed her eyes again and put her head back down on the floor. "In the meantime, you need to not worry about this; you aren't cursed, you just had a string of bad luck."

"Are you sure?"

"Positive," I said.

"Got any cookies in the jar?" she asked, her eyes straying to my ever-full cookie jar.

"Of course," I said. "There are a few lemon shortbread cookies left."

Her eyes lit up. "I love those." As she helped herself to three and sat down at the table, nibbling the first, she said, "Good thing Robert likes women with a little meat on their bones."

"You'd be gorgeous at any weight," I assured her.

"But enough about me... How are things getting on with the botanist?"

"Georgina Krazinsky? She's lovely!" I said. "I'm learning so much!"

"I met her down at the store yesterday," Charlene said. "She was buying chocolate milk; she told me the scientific name of beach roses."

"*Rosa rugosa*?"

"How did you know?"

"She told me yesterday," I said, leaning back and looking out the back window to where several specimens bloomed along the path, scenting the air with their wine-sweet perfume. "Between Georgina and Alex, it's been quite educational around here. I'm kind of surprised she and Alex haven't hit it off; they've got all kinds of naturey, sciencey things in common."

"I know, right? Have they talked at all?"

"They chatted over breakfast this morning, but from what I can tell, he only has eyes for you."

"Only because I'm no longer available." She sighed. "What's she here studying, by the way?"

"The native lupines," I told her. "Evidently the ones we're so famous for were imported from the West Coast a long time ago. There's a children's book about a woman named Mrs. Rumphius who secretly seeded them on her walks." The inn was blessed with a gorgeous stand of the blue and pink flowers; it was a particularly colorful stand that swept from the gray-shingled inn down to the rocky coast and bloomed every spring. My niece Gwen had captured them in watercolor more than once. I'd tried several times myself before reluctantly deciding that my skills were more suited to baking than painting.

"I've seen that book in Sherman's Bookstore," Charlene said. "Was there really a Mrs. Rumphius?"

"There was, but her name was Hilda Edwards, and she may not have been such a hero. Apparently the nonnative lupines have pretty much wiped out the native ones—and the butterflies who relied on them. The original lupines may not have been as showy, but Georgina thinks they're pretty special."

"Are there any native lupines here?"

"She's found a few stands. She doesn't know if they've hybridized with the nonnatives; she's doing DNA testing and collecting seeds. If she can propagate some and store some of the seeds, she says she can help maintain genetic diversity."

"I love our lupines, no matter where they come from."

"Well, apparently the beach roses and purple loosestrife are invasive, too."

"The beach roses? No!"

"Yup. That's why I know they're called *Rosa rugosa*. And that beautiful pink spike flower that grows along I-95 on the way to Portland's bad news, too."

"I love that stuff!"

"So did someone else, which is why it got here." I sighed; it was too bad so many beautiful plants were bad for the local flora and fauna. "I've learned a lot since she's been here, though. It's been a long time since I've gotten to talk about wild plants."

"That's right... you used to work for Texas Parks and Wildlife, didn't you?"

"Indeed I did." In a former life, I had been a cube jockey in a state agency in Texas. I'd enjoyed parts of my work, but not nearly as much as I enjoyed being an innkeeper in Maine.

"Speaking of flowers, did you hear what happened to Ingrid's garden?"

"Claudette's goats on the rampage again?" I asked. Muffin and Pudge, while adorable, were the bane of Ingrid's—and every other gardener on the island's— existence, mowing through gardens like they were bags of potato chips. My window boxes had fallen prey to the dynamic duo more than once.

"Nope. Matilda Jenkins found a diary belonging to a Margaret Selfridge in a box of things Murray dropped off at the museum last week, and there was an entry in there that for some reason nobody's looked at since she wrote it more than fifty years ago."

"What about?"

Charlene leaned forward, eyes sparkling; she loved a good story. "Her husband was one of the Selfridge boys; he was the master of a merchant marine vessel. It was always rumored that he'd brought back a fabulous jewel from one of his trips to the Far East. It was another one of those stories that goes around every once in a while. That there's buried treasure on the island. For some reason, everyone thinks it's somewhere near her house.

"The legends just never stop, do they? Lost pirate ships, rum runners, a ghost at the lighthouse..."

"Well, technically, all of those were kind of true," Charlene pointed out. "It's no wonder treasure hunters dug up her hydrangea bed."

"The beautiful pale blue ones?" I asked. "That's so sad!"

Charlene nodded. "It is... and she's livid."

"I'll bet," I said. "So, what's the story?"

"This time it's some fabulous ruby her husband brought back from the Far East, set in a gold ring. It was supposedly enormous; she wore it for years."

"So showiness runs in the family?" I asked, thinking of the island's current ostentatious Self-ridge, a developer named Murray.

"It seems so. As she got older, she thought someone was going to steal it, so she hid it away. The courtship was passionate, from the stories, but he was gone to sea for months at a time, sometimes years, and even though they had children together, it took its toll on her."

"You had that with your photographer boyfriend."

"Totally," she said. "Except for the marriage and children part, anyway. I'm still mad at him for not making me a priority." She looked out the window, down toward the deep blue water and the gray-green hills of the mainland beyond. "If he'd done things differently... I don't know. I love Robert, but Alex had a zest for life that was really appealing."

"I can see that," I said. I loved Robert, and wanted things to go well with him and Charlene, but I understood where she was coming from.

"Anyway," she said, shaking herself as if to rid herself of bad thoughts, "I can't imagine what it would have been like to be alone for months, not knowing if your husband was alive or dead."

"That's where the widow's walks came from, from what I've heard," I said. One of the captain's houses close to the pier had one; the story was that it was so that the women left behind could climb to the tops of their houses and scan the sea for any sign of their husband's return.

"I've heard that," she said.

"What happened to the ring?" I asked, bringing her back to the story—and, hopefully, away from thoughts of Alex.

"Nobody saw it for years; she'd stopped wearing it. When she died, it was nowhere to be found. Her children asked her what had become of it, but she was suffering from dementia by then, and couldn't tell them anything."

"Helpful."

"Evidently not. It hasn't been seen since years before she died."

"Cheerful story," I remarked.

"Yeah, isn't it? In the past, a lot of these women were lonely if they didn't get involved in island life; their husbands were always gone to sea," Charlene said. "It must have been really stressful."

"You know what that's like, don't you?"

She snorted.

"So, where did she bury it?"

"Oddly, no one can decide on that; everyone's got a different opinion. She was married to William Selfridge."

"Jonah Selfridge's son?" I asked.

"I think so; Matilda told me, but I don't remember exactly which one it was. They lived here, but when she got older, she spent time at her children's houses; they took turns taking care of her. She could have hidden the ring at any number of houses on the island."

"Including the inn," I said, looking out toward the garden. "Terrific. Maybe I should get a metal detector of my own and beat out whoever's looking for it."

"Want me to bring mine?" she asked.

"You have a metal detector?"

"I've been beachcombing for years," she said. "You never know what you'll find after a storm!"

"I think that might be fun; I doubt we'll find

jewels, but maybe we'll find some interesting artifacts!" I said.

"I'll bring it over later."

"If you have a few minutes, I can put on the tea kettle," I suggested.

"He doesn't come into the kitchen, does he?" she asked, looking wary.

"He hasn't so far."

As I spoke, I caught a flash of light outside the window, near the driveway. I bit my lip; it was the sun glancing off the lens of Alex's ever-present camera as he strode down the hill.

"He's here," I said as he spotted Charlene's van. A hungry, hopeful look on his handsome face, he trotted up to the kitchen window and peered in.

Charlene froze, a cookie halfway to her mouth, looking like a deer caught in headlights. He hurried to the door and let himself into the kitchen, along with a burst of fresh spring air. With his good looks, his lean frame, and the eager sparkle in his eye, I could see why Charlene had been drawn to him, but her face now was closed.

"Charlene!" he said. "I was just down at the store looking for you, and it turns out you're here. Did you get the flowers?"

"I did," she said. "But I'm seeing someone. You need to stop."

"I messed up before," he said. "I didn't make you enough of a priority. But things have changed. I want to settle down, share a life with you... maybe even start a family."

At the mention of a family, I saw the set of Charlene's jaw soften, and her eyes looked a bit misty. "But you were never here," she pointed out. "You kept promising..."

"I know," he said, crossing the distance between them. "But things are different now. I quit my job."

"You quit?"

"Last week," he said. "I told them I'm done. I want to settle down, be part of a community. I just can't keep living out of a suitcase all the time."

"Why didn't you do this before?" Charlene asked, swiping at her eyes. "I begged you to stay, but you always said just one more job..."

As I watched, he got down on one knee in front of her and fished in his pocket. "It wasn't until I lost you that I knew what I had. Charlene," he said, producing a sparkling diamond ring. His voice was low and hoarse. "Will you marry me?"

Charlene blinked at him, a half-eaten shortbread cookie in her right hand. As she and Alex stared at each other, there was a shadow at the back window. As I turned to see who it was, there was a knock at the door leading to the front of the inn.

I turned to see my cousin Robert.

~

"Oh, no," Charlene breathed, standing up and wiping crumbs from her shirt. "Put that away," she admonished Alex, hurrying to the door to greet Robert, whose expression was, to put it mildly, stormy.

"Who's this?" he asked.

Before Charlene had a chance to answer, Alex stepped up and extended a hand. "I'm Alex Van der Berg. And you must be my rival for this beautiful woman's affections."

"So you're the one who's been stalking my girlfriend," Robert said.

"Not stalking," Alex said. "I came to visit her."

"I don't believe she invited you," Robert said coolly, "and it's my understanding that she's asked you to leave her alone."

Alex shrugged. "She's angry over what happened between us," he said. "And she should be. I just want to explain..."

"Leave," Robert said in a voice that brooked no discussion.

"Where am I supposed to go? I'm staying at the inn."

"Go to your room then," Robert said. "I don't care

where you go, as long as it isn't here. If the lady has told you to leave her alone, you need to respect her request."

Alex put his hands up. "No offense meant," he said. "I'll leave now." Before he turned to go, his eyes shot to Charlene. "Think about it," he told her, then walked to the door and let himself out quietly.

"Think about what?" Robert asked when he'd gone.

"It's nothing," Charlene said, her eyes darting away from his. "I'm so glad you're here." She planted a kiss on his cheek, but I couldn't help noticing that there was a distracted air to the gesture.

"What happened?" Robert asked.

Charlene sighed. "He just proposed to me."

Robert blinked. "Proposed? What did you say?"

"You turned up before I had a chance to answer," she said. Then, after a pause, she added, "The answer is no, of course."

Robert's face flushed, and his eyes glinted with anger. "He asked you to marry him?"

Charlene nodded.

"What a jerk," Robert said, shaking his head. "He can't be bothered to stop by for six months at a time, and now that you've let him go and started another relationship, he wants to pull you back in."

"He is a jerk," I concurred.

"I just wish he'd never come back," Charlene said, stuffing the rest of the cookie into her mouth. "I'm surprised to see you, sweetheart; I thought you weren't here until this coming weekend!"

"I took a few days off," Robert said. "The weather's lovely, and I wanted to spend it with you."

"That's so romantic," she said, leaning over to give him a kiss.

"Tania said you'd come up to the inn. I wanted to surprise you; I guess I succeeded."

"You got here just in time," she said. "I've got to head back to the store; want to come with me?"

"I'd love to," he said. I watched as the two left the kitchen, hands linked as they headed for Charlene's truck, and couldn't help feeling a frisson of worry. Robert was a good man; he was solid, handsome, and loved Charlene completely. But he didn't have the rakish looks or sense of adventure of her former flame, and I had a bad feeling that, despite her protestations, she still harbored feelings for the wayward photographer.

Not for the first time, I wished Alex had stayed out with the whales in the San Juan Islands, or wherever he was, as long as it wasn't here.

∽

I was just finishing another batch of lemon shortbread cookies when there was a knock at the door. It was Matilda Jenkins, the town historian and keeper of the museum.

"Hey!" I said, opening the door and welcoming her in. "I hear you made an exciting discovery this week!"

"I did," she said. "And since you live in one of the Selfridges' houses, I thought you might be interested, too, so I made a copy of the diary for you."

"That's so sweet!" I said. "Want a cookie?" I offered. "They just came out of the oven."

"I'd love one," she said, sitting down at the kitchen table. As I set out a few cookies on a plate, she pulled a stack of copies from her purse and spread them out on the table.

"Margaret's diary?" I inquired as I sat down next to her, taking in the spidery writing.

"It is," she said. "I just wish I had more information about which house she was living in at the time."

"Nobody knows?"

"She moved around from one child's house to another," she said. "They shared the burden of caring for her as she started to decline."

"That's what Charlene said. And you don't know where she was at the end?"

"No," she said. "She doesn't say. She just talks

about pirates coming, and burying her valuables "where the wolves gather to gaze out at Gull Rock."

I leaned over her shoulder to look at the spidery, erratic handwriting.

"Wolves? There aren't any wolves on Cranberry Island."

"She was struck with dementia at the end," Matilda reminded me. "The thing is, I made the mistake of telling Emmeline about this. Now the whole island knows; I even got a call from Gertrude from the *Daily Mail*."

"Oh, no," I said. "Everyone's going to be digging for the famous ruby ring now. Was that really a thing, by the way?"

"I have a photo of her wearing it," she said. "Right here." She pulled out a photo of a pretty young woman in a long, old-fashioned dress, standing stiff-backed next to a man with a beard and a suit. On her hand, which was held at an angle in front of her, was what appeared to be a massive ring. Behind them, I recognized the shingles of the inn; it was odd, seeing these strangers in a picture of the place I now called home. It was once theirs, I realized, and wondered what these walls had seen over the years.

"Is that William Selfridge with her?"

"One of Murray's ancestors, yes. He brought the ring back for her. She was supposed to marry someone else, but he managed to woo her away... this giant ruby was part of it. She wore it long after he died at sea, apparently... only in the last few years did she start having paranoia about pirates."

"So she hid it."

"She did," Matilda confirmed. "She supposedly buried the ring and the rest of her jewelry. But no one knows where."

"Well, we do now," I said.

"Right," Matilda said dryly. "Where the wolves get together to look at Gull Rock."

"Gull Rock's right off the island. Anyone on the island named Wolf?" I asked.

"Not that I know of," she said, "but I'll double-check the records. That's a good idea."

"Are people really digging up gardens at all the old Selfridge residences?"

"They are," she said. "Ingrid lost her hydrangeas and Emmeline found a bunch of kids digging around her veggie garden. You haven't had anyone here yet?"

"Not that I know of," I said. "But I'm sure they'll be coming, especially if Gertrude publishes something about it." I groaned; that was all I needed... half of Mount Desert Island treasure-hunting in the front yard of the inn.

"Wait," she said. "There was a Wolf family from

Germany here at some point; I remember seeing it in census."

"What year?" I asked.

"I don't know," she said. "I'll have to research it."

"If you can find out where they lived, at least that might distract some of the diggers."

"I'll get on it," I said. "In the meantime, do you want me to leave this here? Maybe you can make something of it."

"I'd love that," I said. "It's always fun seeing how people lived in the past."

"It is, isn't it?" she asked, lighting up. "There's so much hidden history all around it; it's wonderful just thinking about it. That's why I work in the museum; it brings the past to life for me, at least in some small way, every day."

"I often think about all the people who lived here before me," I said, touching one of the inn's walls. How many women had cooked in this kitchen? How many pies and loaves of bread had been baked here, how many dinners made for hungry families? "Thanks for bringing this by," I said, my mind still sifting through thoughts of the past as I riffled the copied pages of a diary almost a century ago. One passage in particular stuck out to me: *William has been gone for 273 days now, and I have no way of knowing if he is alive or dead. I walk down to the shore every day, searching the horizon. His last missive arrived three months ago. He has been silent too long, I fear.*

"You said her husband died at sea?" I asked, looking up at Matilda.

"He did," she said. "It was very sad. His ship went down somewhere off the Grand Banks; he last made port in England. Apparently she got his last letter just before she found out the ship went down, and all hands were lost. It's here," she said, flipping to the end of the stack of pages. "It's no wonder it's said the house was cursed for the Selfridges. His father, and then William."

Dearest Margaret, the letter began. *I write this to you from London. It has been a long and lonely journey, although successful; with luck, only a few more such voyages and I will be able to remain in your loving arms forever. I cannot wait to hold you again, and to see your sweet smile. I dream of you picking lupines in the spring, the roses in your cheeks, your hair flying in the wind, and of the sound of small feet rushing down the front stairs to the parlor, of you cradling our infant in your soft arms.*

In the meantime, I have acquired two volumes of botanical prints, which I trust you will love, including yet another treatise on the identification and uses of flowering plants.

"So romantic. They were really in love, weren't they?"

"They were," Matilda confirmed. "It's very sweet... and very tragic. She was apparently very interested in plants, and was something of a healer on the island."

"No wonder he was bringing her books. How thoughtful!" I said, glancing over the description of the house in the letter again. "This sounds like the inn," I said.

"It does, doesn't it?" she said.

"Are there lupines?"

"Not now, but who knows what there was back then?"

I glanced out the window at the swathe of lupines leading down to the rocky coast as Matilda finished her cookie. "How long did they live here?"

"I'm not sure," she said. "She and her husband lived here when they were first married, but I don't know when she started moving to stay with extended family. There were bedrooms on the first floor, but it must have been a lot to keep up for a widow, I imagine."

"The place was in pretty bad shape when I bought it, but she'd been long gone by then. There's so much history I don't know about this old place," I said, looking at the yellow walls of my kitchen and thinking of all they had seen over the years.

"Any more ghost sightings?" she asked.

"Not since we solved the mystery of what happened," I said. A few years back, we'd had a specter at the inn; once we'd uncovered the cause of her death, she seemed to have been satisfied, and we hadn't heard from her since. I always wondered if Annie was still around... or if there were other ghosts here I hadn't yet encountered.

"Strange business," she commented.

"It is," I said. "I didn't used to believe, but now..."

"There are more things in heaven and earth..." Matilda said, and a little shiver crept down my spine.

∽

John went to bed early, but I stayed up late that night, folding laundry and thinking about the ruby myth. Was there in fact a huge ruby floating around the island? I wondered if Margaret had lied about burying it and actually sold it. Were "the wolves" a reference to greedy relatives? And if so, where might they have gathered?

When I finished the laundry, I assembled the ingredients for Chocolate Walnut Sea Salt Caramel Bars; I was craving something sweet, and had been dying to try the recipe. I softened the butter in the microwave, then set to work creaming the butter and adding in brown sugar and flour; I could almost taste the crust already as I pressed it into a foil-lined pan and put it into the oven. As I was measuring out chocolate and unwrapping caramels for the topping, I heard the front door open and close. Curious, I headed to the parlor, wondering who was out so late, but by the time I got there, whoever it was had already disappeared up the stairs. I heard a door close on the second floor above me. Since all my guests were on the second floor, there was no way to know who it was; I did, however, notice a bit of fresh dirt and grass smudged on the front carpet.

I cleaned it up with a few paper towels, buffing out the mud, and then followed the tracks up the stairs, picking up bits of dirt and grass as I went. By the time I got to the top step, however, the dirt had worn off. There was one muddy bit of grass on the runner in the hallway leading toward where both Alex and Georgina were housed, but even a close examination of the rug in front of their doors didn't reveal who had been out. Had someone had insomnia and gone for a walk? Or had Alex made a late night visit to Charlene and Robert? If so, I mused, I'd find out about it in the morning.

Why was I so worried about it, anyway? I wondered as I headed back downstairs; the timer on my phone had started beeping, and it was time to take the pan out of the oven. The digging must have me on edge; it bothered me to know someone was on the property without my knowing it. I retreated to the kitchen, pulled the pan from the oven and spread chocolate chips on it, covering the pan with foil so that the chocolate would melt. While the pan rested, I turned on the back porch light, grabbed my flashlight and headed out to the back yard. I swept the area with my light, but saw no sign of additional activity. Then I looked up at the inn. Both Alex and Georgina were still up; there were lights in both rooms, so there was no way to know who had been out and about.

I sighed and headed back inside, still wondering who had been out—and why—as I smoothed the melted chocolate over the crust, then put the caramels into a bowl with cream and put them into the microwave to melt. When the caramel was melted, I spread it over the chocolate, then finished it with walnuts and a sprinkling of sea salt, allowing myself one warm corner before heading up to join John. It was crumbly and gooey and melty and delicious, and it was all I could do not to wolf down half the pan.

Resisting the urge to dig into the cooling bar cookies again, I covered them with foil and headed upstairs to John. He was already asleep, and the cats, Biscuit, and Smudge, who were thoughtfully warming my pillow for me. Biscuit meowed as I crawled into bed, snuggling into me, and Smudge took up residence by my right ear; their purring soon soothed me to sleep.

∽

"How's the hunt?" I asked the next morning as Georgina came down to breakfast, a laptop under one arm and a basket slung over the other. She was a fit, attractive woman, her dark hair pulled back and only a touch of make-up on her chiseled features. Today she wore a pair of slim jeans that flattered her slender figure and an indigo blouse that dove rather deep; above it was a crystal pendant shaped like her favorite flower, the lupine.

"I've found three stands," she said, "and about six scattered individuals. I'm collecting leaves for genetic analysis, but I'm going to have to come back to collect seed once the blooming period is over. But I found something even more interesting."

"What?" I asked.

"Some of the lupines I took from your property are genetically different from the others."

"Oh, really?"

"Yes," she said. "They have a mutation that I'm not seeing in the populations on the mainland, and it's concentrated in the plants around your inn. It's like they're a separate population, somehow... planted earlier, or in isolation."

"Weird," I said.

"It is. I wish I could get to the bottom of it." She glanced around the dining room. "Is the nature photographer down yet?"

"I haven't seen him," I said as I poured her a cup of coffee. "You two have a lot in common, it seems."

"Oh, we do," she said. "I was hoping I could get him to take a few photos of the lupines in bloom. I got a few pics on my phone, but they're not exactly magazine-worthy."

"You could ask," I said. "I don't think he's here on a job."

"I heard... something about a woman on the island? Charlotte, or something?"

"Charlene," I said. "They were dating for a while, but broke up a few months ago."

"Why is he here, then?"

"Hope springs eternal?" I said. No need to mention the details.

She played with a strand of her hair. "If she broke up with him a few months ago, he must not be too into her."

"I'm afraid I can't comment. He is handsome,

though; you two would make a good match, with your interest in science."

"What... me?" she said, flushing. "I'd never thought about that."

The roses in her cheeks and the sparkle in her eyes made me think otherwise.

"Worth asking him to dinner," I suggested.

"Huh. That's a good idea."

"I'd be happy to make something here, if you like. I can even find a bottle of wine. "

"Would you?" she asked. "I'll just wait for him to come down, then," she said. "What's for breakfast, anyway?"

"Migas," I told her.

"I haven't had those since I visited Austin a few years back." She took a sip of coffee and plugged in her computer. "I'd gain fifty pounds in a year if I had your job."

"Oh, you work off a lot of it, I promise you," I told her. "I'll go get breakfast started."

"Thanks," she said, flipping open her computer. I caught a glimpse of the web page she had open as I turned back to the kitchen; it was Alex's Facebook page. She was obviously more interested in him than she'd let on. I hoped he'd be willing to have dinner with her. If nothing else, maybe it would distract him from his pursuit of Charlene.

It didn't take me long to assemble the migas, a favorite from my home state of Texas that was a delicious mix of eggs, garlic, onion, tortilla chip pieces and just a touch of jalapeño (for northern palates). I was serving it alongside link sausage and a fruit salad made with chopped melon and fresh blueberries I'd picked just yesterday. Even after years of living in Maine, there was still something wonderful about berry picking, and I still made time for it.

Alex had come down by the time I returned to the dining room with a plate for Georgina.

"I think I've met you before," she was saying to the handsome photographer, who was standing next to her table. She was leaning toward him, her head tilted at a coquettish angle, a strand of dark hair falling over her cheek. "At the endangered species conference in Denver last year. You told me you always had a thing for brunettes, remember?'

He glanced at me, and unless I was mistaken, a faint blush colored his cheeks.

"I meant to ask you yesterday," she continued, "but our paths never crossed."

"I was busy," he said vaguely.

"Anyway, I was hoping I'd convince you to come and take some photos for me. I'm submitting an article to *Discover Magazine*, and having your photos would just make it shine."

"Photos of what?" he asked as I put the plate down in front of Georgina. She barely noticed; it was obvious that Alex had worked his charms on yet another hapless victim.

"Lupines," she said, in a breathy voice that made me want to roll my eyes

"I usually rely more on the fauna side of the nature equation," he said, not convinced.

"Oh, these are special lupines," she said. "Endangered."

"Are they?" he asked. "How do you know about them?"

"I'm a science writer and researcher," she said. "Sit down and I'll tell you all about it."

"Go ahead," I encouraged him. "I'll bring breakfast out in a minute."

"Is Charlene going to be here this morning?" he asked. At the mention of my friend's name, a shadow passed over Georgina's face.

"Who's Charlene?" she asked.

"His ex-girlfriend," I answered for him, even though I knew Georgina already knew about her. Alex's mouth tightened before opening as if to contradict me, but I kept going. "You two get acquainted; I'm sure you'll find you have a lot in common. I'll be back with your breakfast shortly." And before he could protest, I high-tailed it to the kitchen.

I'd just returned from delivering breakfast to what I hoped would soon be lovebirds when John came downstairs, smelling of soap and the wonderful woodsy aroma that was uniquely his.

"Hey, were you doing some gardening yesterday?"

"No," I said. "Why?"

"When I opened the curtains, I noticed it looks like someone's been plowing up the bed by the roses," he said.

I groaned. "The treasure hunters have found us."

As I spoke, the phone rang. I was about to grab it when I saw the caller ID; it was Gertrude Pickens, the intrepid (and very nosy) reporter from the *Daily Mail*.

"Don't answer that!" I warned John as he reached for it.

"Why?"

I related the new hidden treasure story that was going around the island. "Matilda dropped off a copy of her diary yesterday. It looks like Margaret did bury it somewhere around here, and she lived here for at least part of the time, so there's a chance we've got a giant ruby somewhere on the property."

"Wouldn't it belong to her heirs if it was found?"

"You mean like Murray?"

"He doesn't really need a ruby, does he?" John mused.

"No. But I guess it could, if he could prove it belonged to his ancestor," I said. "But if it's on our property, wouldn't it be ours if someone found it?"

"If people are digging under cover of night, they're probably not going to announce where they found something valuable, are they?" John pointed out.

"Probably not," I agreed. "Charlene was going to come over with her metal detector, but with Alex here... Speaking of Charlene, she's been getting some nasty poisoned pen letters."

John's face took on a serious cast. "Any threats?"

"Not directly, but it's upsetting."

"Tell her to save them; I want to take a look at them. Maybe we should go over to pick up the detector, and I can take a look at what she's been sent."

"I'm hoping Georgina can convince Alex to go take pictures of lupines today so Charlene can come here... I suggested Georgina invite Alex to dinner, too. Maybe that'll keep him from stalking Charlene."

"Has Charlene considered a restraining order?" he asked.

"All he's done is leave flowers on her doorstep and propose to her," I said. "Does that qualify?"

"I doubt it, but I'll look into it," he promised. "I'm headed down to assess the damage, then do a bit of work in my workshop, but I'll take care of the dishes after breakfast, okay?"

"Sounds like a plan," I said as he poured himself a cup of coffee. He gave me a quick kiss and headed out the back door, and once again I thanked my lucky stars that I'd married him.

∽

I had just finished making a second pot of coffee when the phone rang. It was Charlene.

"That jerk."

"What?"

"Someone left a pile of goat poop on my doorstep. With a nice note calling me a five-letter word starting with 'w.'" She paused for a moment. "And the word wasn't widow. I'll send you a pic."

My phone buzzed, and a picture of what she had described popped up on the screen, complete with a note, the letters in the same block print as the last one. Again, the 'w' had curved bottoms and a graceful flourish at the top completely at odds with the stark nastiness of the word.

"Classy," I said. "Any ideas?"

"Do you think it could be Alex?" she asked.

"What? I thought he was trying to woo you!"

"He is, but I think he's mad I'm with someone else," she said.

"I'm still guessing it might be your earlier letter writer. Could it be Fern? Robert just came into town, after all; maybe she's upset that he's staying with you?"

"It could be," she said. "She did come down to the store yesterday, come to think of it. She didn't look happy when Robert gave me a hug."

"On the other hand, if it was Alex, that would explain the person who came in tracking mud at 11:30 last night," I said. "Although maybe it wasn't mud."

"If I wasn't already over him, I am now," she pronounced, but I still heard that note of doubt in her voice.

"Where's Robert?" I asked.

"In the shower," she said. "He's going to hang out at the store with me, in case Alex decides to come back."

"You know you're doing the right thing, don't you?" I asked.

"I guess," she said. "It was a lot of fun to be with him, though."

"It was, for about 21 days a year," I said.

She sighed. "So true. He's a fantasy, isn't he?"

"He is," I confirmed. "Much better to have someone you can share your life with."

"It's the day-to-day that makes a relationship worthwhile, isn't it?"

"Having someone who's there for you," I said, thinking of John.

"I guess you're right. Anyway, I've got to run," she said.

"Let me know if anything else happens, okay?" I asked.

"Of course."

I poured myself another cup of coffee and decided to let Alex and Georgina have a few minutes alone before I headed back into the dining room. As I propped my feet up on the chair across from me, I spied the copied pages Matilda had dropped off the day before. I grabbed them and began leafing through them.

William returned from a voyage to California, she had written in one entry. *He brought me a lovely white spiked flower with a pod that is oddly inflated, like a bladder. It grows next to the sea, so it is possible it might survive the coast here. I will attempt to germinate the seeds, but they are small and I am not hopeful.* I read on; between entries about the weather and her missing William, she wrote about her garden and the botanical oddities her husband brought her from around the world. He supplied her with seeds and plants from all his travels, it seemed, both pressed and preserved, from many ports of call. I wondered what had happened to her botanical collection.

Margaret was a talented writer, and quite a botanist, it seemed. And her husband was happy to bring her all manner of books and specimens from his travels; he apparently pressed the leaves of several unusual specimens, and even brought her back a cactus or two.

I thought about Charlene and her former beau, Alex. Like them, Margaret and William hadn't spent much time together, but it was obvious from the notes of Margaret's diary that it wasn't by choice; they had a deep and abiding relationship, and although I did not have her letters to him, she referenced them often in her diary.

As coffee brewed, I turned to a page that mentioned lupines.

The name, he tells me, is Lupinus, or big-leafed lupine, and it is a tall, regal flower with purple and pink spikes. I look forward to trying them in the meadow below the house, not far from the roses along the path. It resembles a flower I've seen on the island, a legume from the pods and the leaves, but larger. The name is intriguing and I plan to research it.

My mind whirled as I stood up. Georgina had said the lupines on the island had a different genetic make-up from the ones on the mainland. Could it be because the population was started by Margaret long before the plants were brought to the mainland? Did Cranberry Island have its own Mrs. Rumphius?

I marked the pages with a slip of paper and headed out to the dining room, hoping Georgina would still be there.

She wasn't; both she and Alex had vacated the dining room. Since she hadn't asked me to cook dinner, I was guessing her invitation hadn't been accepted—or if it had, they'd decided on the co-op.

Georgina's laptop was gone, but Alex's camera was still on the table. Which was weird, since he never traveled without the thing; Charlene always used to say he liked the camera more than her. Georgina's breakfast had barely been touched, and there was a fork on the floor, along with some migas, as if it had been knocked there accidentally.

As I bent down to pick up the fork, I spotted a notebook open on the floor beside Georgina's chair. It was a list of locations, presumably of lupine stands. She must have left it behind accidentally.

As I picked up the notebook, the name Southwest Harbor jumped out at me.

Not the name.

One of the letters in the name.

My stomach lurched as I hurried out of the dining room into the parlor. There was no sign of them.

What had happened while I was in the kitchen?

I raced to the kitchen and threw open the back door, running down to the workshop at top speed. John looked up, startled, when I burst in.

"What's wrong?" he asked, putting down the chisel he'd been using to transform a chunk of driftwood into a whale.

"Georgina is the one who was leaving nasty notes for Charlene," I said.

"How do you know?"

"I recognized the handwriting in her notebook," I told him. "It matches the letters Charlene got. I think Georgina's obsessed with Alex. I left her in the dining room with Alex, but when I went back, his camera was there but they were gone."

"He never goes anywhere without his camera," John said.

"Exactly. I think she may have forced him to go somewhere. They weren't in the dining room or the parlor. I was about to go upstairs, but I came to get you."

"I'm glad you did," he said. He retrieved a two-by-four from the stack in the corner of the workshop and gave it an experimental swing. "Let's go."

Together we ran back up to the inn. I showed him the scene in the dining room. "You're right. They left in a hurry," he confirmed.

"We should check upstairs," I said.

"That was my thought."

Together, we hurried up the stairs to the second story. "Which rooms are they in?" he asked in a low voice.

"She's in the Lupine room," I told him.

"Of course she is," he said. "Stay behind me," he said, and I was happy to oblige; after all, I wasn't the one carrying the two-by-four.

As we approached the Lupine Room, I could hear voices.

"She's not your type," Georgina was saying in a rather whiny tone. "You need someone who's into the same kinds of things you are. When we met, I knew we were meant to be together."

"I don't even know you," Alex was saying. "Please. Put that away."

"No," she said. "Now. Tell me what you're looking for in a woman."

"I... well, someone who isn't threatening me, for starters."

"I'm not threatening you," she purred. "I'm making sure you notice me."

"It's working," he said. "Now... can we put that aside, please? I'd like to get closer, but I don't feel comfortable with you holding that."

John and I exchanged glances. If she was holding a gun on him, breaking down the door wasn't a good idea. John shook his head; we both stayed frozen.

"Don't you think you can trust me?" she asked.

"Of course I think I can trust you," Alex said. "It's just... uncomfortable. I don't want to shift and make it go off or something." He was quiet for a moment, then, in a voice like melted chocolate, said, "Georgina. Trust me."

After a pause during which I held my breath, she relented. "All right," she said. There was a soft clunk —a gun being set on a table?—and then silence for a moment.

Then I heard Alex say, "Isn't that better?"

"It is," Georgina said in a simpering voice. "I told you in Denver we'd make a good match. Why didn't you listen?"

"I was... distracted," he said.

"What are you doing?" she asked sharply.

There was a cracking sound from inside the room, then Georgina shrieked, "Alex! No!"

John tried to turn the knob; the door was locked. He motioned to me to back up, then kicked the door in with one blow.

Inside, Alex had grabbed the gun and was pointing it at Georgina, who looked like she was about to launch herself at him from the bed. Both turned, startled, as John barreled into the room, two-by-four in hand.

"It's not what it looks like," Alex said quickly. "She pulled the gun out of her purse at breakfast and forced me to come up here."

"I know," I said. "We heard through the door."

"You ruined it," Georgina said to John and me through gritted teeth. Then she turned on Alex. "You said I could trust you. You're a liar, is what you are. A liar. I wish I'd never met you, Alex Van der Berg."

"The feeling, madam," Alex said as he relinquished the gun to John, "is mutual."

∽

The mainland police were on the spot within a half hour, and we weren't unhappy to see Georgina go.

"I can't believe she stalked me here," Alex said as we had a cup of coffee at the inn's kitchen table. He'd retrieved his camera, and kept reaching out to touch it, as if he were afraid it might vanish. "Apparently she's had a mad crush on me since that conference. I got a few e-mails from some woman online, but I just kind of ignored them; I didn't realize it was the same person."

"You didn't recognize her?"

"There are a lot of people at conferences," he said, and shivered. "It's weird to think she was stalking me."

"Speaking of stalking," I commented, "don't you think it might be time to let Charlene go?"

He blinked. "Stalking? You think I'm stalking her?"

"She's dating someone else, but you show up on the island, you follow her around, you keep leaving her flowers, and you've asked her to marry her."

"But she was my girlfriend! That's different!"

"Do you really want to move to Cranberry Island full-time?"

"Well... maybe not full-time," he said, his eyes not meeting mine.

"Let her go," I said.

"But I love her," he protested.

"You had her for a year, and you only showed up to see her a few times."

"I was busy," he said.

"Let her go," I repeated.

"I'll think about it," he said, draining his coffee. "I'm going to go shoot some photos while it's still light. Thanks for the coffee—and thanks to you and your husband for helping me out."

"You're welcome," I said. He left his coffee mug on the table and sauntered out the door, leaving me to wonder what Georgina had seen in him. Other than good looks, there wasn't much there, from what I could see, except for a selfish little boy who hadn't grown up.

At least Georgina hadn't killed him in the Lupine Room, though.

Speaking of lupines, I reached again for Georgina's notebook. There were two species names written on the first page: *Lupinus polyphyllus* and *Lupinus perennis*. We had a smaller lupine of our own in Texas—*Lupinus texensis*, the Texas Bluebonnet. Named after...

"Wolves," I said. "*Lupus* is Latin for wolf." And the stand of lupines at the inn seemed to have a different origin from the other lupines in the state, which had arrived in the 20th century. I grabbed my phone and headed out the back door toward the stand of lupines on the meadow below the inn, and looked out to the water. Sure enough, there in front of me was Gull Rock.

I called Charlene. "Do you have that metal detector?"

"It's in the truck," she said. "I was going to bring it over later."

"Can you bring it now? I think I know where that ruby is. And I've got some other news, too."

"Hang on," she said, and I heard talking in the background. "Robert will mind the store; I'll be right over. Is Alex there?"

"No," I said. "He went out to take pictures somewhere."

"Whew," she said. "I'll see you in a few."

Fifteen minutes later, Charlene appeared, carrying a metal detector. I got up from the slab of granite I'd been sitting on and walked to greet her.

"What's going on?" she asked.

"First, let me fill you in on Alex and Georgina," I said. I related the goings-on at the inn... everything but my request to Alex to leave Charlene alone.

"She stalked him here?"

"Yes... and she sent you the nasty letters," I said. "I recognized the 'w' from the two letters you showed me."

"Sounds like someone's got some serious mental health issues," Charlene said with a shudder. "And she had a gun, too?"

"It wasn't loaded, but yes," I said. "The police took her away a little while ago."

"Good," Charlene said. "But that doesn't explain the metal detector."

"Before she went crazy, Georgina told me that the lupines near the inn are different genetically from the ones on the mainland... and on the rest of the island. I think it's because Margaret's husband brought back lupine seeds for her at the end of the 19th century, and she planted them here."

"So?"

"So... in her diary, she said she hid the ruby where the wolves gather to look at Gull Rock."

"There aren't any wolves on the island," Charlene said.

"No," I said. "But the name for lupines comes from wolves. *Lupinus* comes from the Latin word for wolf: *lupus*."

"Weird," Charlene said, looking at the swath of purple and pink flowers. "They look nothing like wolves."

"They think the flowers were named that because people thought they "wolfed" up nutrients from the soil. Margaret had a lot of botanical knowledge. She must have known the meaning of the name."

Charlene's eyes widened. "So when she was

talking about the wolves gathering, you think she meant the lupines!"

"Yes," I said. "I'm hoping she meant the ones she planted, and I'm hoping your metal detector will help us find it."

"Do you get to keep it if we do?"

"Let's find it first. Then we'll worry about who it belongs to." I glanced over at my decimated roses. If we were successful, I hoped it would at least bring an end to prospecting in my garden.

"Here goes," Charlene said, and turned on the detector, carefully stepping around the blooming lupines as she scanned the meadow.

After ten minutes, it beeped. "I've got something," she said.

"Let me get a trowel from the shed," I said. I hurried down to the garden shed and returned a few minutes later with both a trowel and a shovel. She pointed to the spot, and I dug until I felt the trowel's blade clink against something.

"What is it?" Charlene asked as I felt in the moist soil. A moment later, I retrieved a bit of rusted metal.

"Not a ruby," I said. "See if there's anything else?"

She ran the detector over the spot again, but got nothing.

"I'll keep trying," she said.

We had three more false alarms and were about to give up when the detector beeped again. It was a few feet from the rock I'd been sitting on.

"Got another hit," Charlene said.

I dug with the trowel, but found nothing.

"Try the shovel," my friend suggested. I did, and had gotten about eighteen inches in when I hit something hard.

I used the trowel to clear the rest of the dirt from what looked to be a small box made of wood; it was about the size and shape of a cigar box. I pried it out of the soil with the trowel and set it down on the rock. It wasn't locked, but the latch was rusted and wouldn't budge. I gave it a few knocks with the trowel before it popped open.

I lifted the lid; inside were several cloth pouches, the material damp and rotting.

"I think we found something," Charlene said, reaching for a pouch and opening the drawstring, pouring the contents onto her palm. A pair of blue gemstone earrings glittered against her pale skin.

"I think you're right," I said. The second pouch contained what appeared to be a pendant encrusted with emeralds. And the third was a ring.

"Bingo," Charlene said, admiring what appeared to be a large, oval ruby flanked by smaller diamonds. "I think we found the buried treasure."

"Let's put it in the box and get back to the inn," I said. "I'll let John know, and we can figure out where to go from here."

As Charlene replaced the pouches in the box, I looked out toward Gull Rock. How many times had Margaret stood here staring out to sea, praying for the return of her husband?

I could only imagine her despair when she learned he had been lost at sea, and would never come back again.

~

It was a week before we heard the results from the appraiser. Alex had left the inn without saying goodbye to either Charlene or me, and I hoped we'd seen the last of him. Georgina, apparently, was out on bail, although I hadn't seen her; she'd gone back home, according to the police.

"Well, the gem is six carats," John announced when he got off the phone.

"Is it?" I asked. "Is it worth a fortune?"

"Depends on what you call a fortune," he said. "It's not a ruby."

"What? It's a fake?"

"It's a stone called a spinel," he said.

"So it's a fake."

"Yes and no," he told me. "For a long time, possibly including when William Selfridge purchased it, a spinel was apparently considered the same as a ruby. So while it may not be as valuable as a ruby now, it still has considerable worth."

"Like how much?"

"Twenty-thousand dollars."

"Holy moly," I said. "And who does it belong to?"

"That's still up in the air," he said. "It was found on our property, but there is some provenance. I let Murray know we found it; he said he would like it to go to the museum, but he'd like to hold onto the necklace. He's offering you the earrings as a finders' fee."

"That's remarkably nice of him," I said. Although they weren't anywhere near as big as the ruby, it would be lovely to have something that belonged to one of the previous inhabitants. "We could always use extra money," I said, "but I don't really feel right selling the ring and keeping the money."

"I think the museum is the right call," he said.

"You know what? I do, too," I said. "If they keep it as an exhibit and publicize the story behind it, it might bring more trade to the island."

"That's true," he said. "And for once, we might like something Gertrude writes about us."

"Forget Gertrude. This is a scoop worthy of the Portland paper... maybe even Boston!"

As I spoke, the phone rang. John glanced at the Caller ID. "It's Gertrude again."

"Do we get in her good graces by giving her first dibs?"

"We'll send press releases to everyone at the same time," he said, then cocked an eyebrow at me. "Do you know how to write a press release?"

"Let me call Murray first," I said.

"I never thought I'd hear you volunteer to call Murray Selfridge," John commented.

"I know, right?" Within fifteen minutes, everything was arranged. Murray and I were donating Margaret's ring to the Cranberry Island Historical Museum. I had just left a message for Matilda when there was a knock at the door.

"Everyone's psychic this morning," John said at the sight of our local historian.

"What's the word?" she asked as I opened the door, letting in both Matilda and a rush of cool spring air. "Did you hear back from the appraiser?"

"We did," I told her. "It's not a real ruby."

"Oh," she said, crestfallen. "I guess William lied to her, or bought a pig in a poke."

"He didn't," I said.

"It's a spinel," John explained. "In the 1800s, it

would be considered a ruby. In fact, the appraiser told me there's a famous one called the Black Prince's Ruby in the U.K."

"So he didn't lie!" Matilda said.

"Turns out he really did put his money where his mouth was," I said. "It's worth twenty-thousand dollars."

Her eyes widened. "What are you going to do with it?" she asked. "I'd love to buy it for the museum, but we could never afford that. Besides," she said, eyes clouding, "Murray wouldn't give it up to you without a fight."

"Not to me, maybe," I said, "but we've both decided to gift it to the museum."

She blinked. "What?"

"We're giving it to you," I repeated. "Maybe you can do a whole exhibit; it might generate some good traffic."

"Oh, it definitely will!" she said. "We can get in touch with the press..."

"We were just talking about that," John said. "Do you know how to write press releases?"

She cocked her head. "I wrote grant applications for twenty years. Of course I can write a press release!"

"We were trying to decide if we should give Gertrude the scoop..." I trailed off.

"After all the things she's printed about you? No way. I've got a contact at the *Boston Globe*... we'll give it to the big boys, first. Maybe even do a traveling exhibit! This really might put us on the map..."

She was off and running. John and I exchanged a fond smile as Matilda made plans. "We'll have to get a secure display space, of course..."

"I can build a case," John offered.

"Oh, that would be perfect. And since you found it here, we'll have to put up a marker and send visitors to see it! I'll bet you'll get some extra guests once they learn the romantic story!"

"I just made a batch of chocolate-caramel walnut bars," I said. "Why don't I make some tea and we can dig in and celebrate?"

"I'd love that," Matilda said. "Walnuts are my favorite!"

As I filled the teakettle and loaded a plate with cookies, Matilda and John sketched out plans for a case. I glanced outside toward Gull Rock, thinking of all the days Margaret had spent looking out to sea, and said a prayer of thanks that I hadn't married a man who made his living at sea.

The Gray Whale Inn might have been cursed for the Selfridges, I reflected as I turned on the stove and bit into one of the buttery, gooey walnut bars, but for me, it had been nothing from a blessing. As I popped the rest of the walnut bar into my mouth and carried the plate to the table, John reached out to touch my arm.

"These look great. Thank you," he said, and his smile made my heart expand until it felt the size of the entire island. I sent a small prayer that Margaret and William were happy somewhere in the great beyond and sat down with my husband and my friend at the big pine table, thankful for the little moments that made life worthwhile.

CHOCOLATE SEA SALT CARAMEL WALNUT BARS

INGREDIENTS

- 1 cup butter, softened
- 1/2 cup firmly packed brown sugar
- 2 cups flour
- 8 oz. semi-sweet chocolate chips
- 12 oz. caramels (unwrapped)
- 1/4 cup whipping cream
- 1 cup chopped walnuts
- 1/2-1 tsp. sea salt (fine or coarse, to taste)

DIRECTIONS

Preheat oven to 350°F. Line a 15x10x3/4-inch

baking pan with foil. with ends of foil extending over sides of pan, and spray with cooking spray.

Cream butter and sugar in a large bowl with electric mixer on medium speed until light and fluffy. Add flour slowly, beating on low speed until mixture is well blended and crumbly. Press dough firmly into pan and bake for 15 to 17 minutes or until edges are golden brown.

Remove pan from oven and sprinkle crust with chocolate chips; cover with foil. Let stand 5 minutes or until chocolate chips are melted, then spread evenly over crust.

Microwave caramels and cream in microwaveable bowl on medium 4 minutes, stirring once at 2 minutes, until caramels begin to melt. Stir until caramels are completely melted. Spread caramel evenly over chocolate layer and sprinkle with walnuts, then sprinkle with sea salt. Cool on pan on wire rack; when cool, remove from pan using foil as handles.

Cut into 36 bars.

<<<<>>>>

ALTAR FLOWERS

ALTAR FLOWERS

It was a bright June afternoon when I ducked into the dark interior of St. James' Episcopal Church, my arms full of blue and pink lupines from the field behind the Gray Whale Inn. As I arranged them in one of the altar vases, a quiet voice startled me.

"I love lupines."

I whirled around, almost dropping the vase. In the front pew sat a wizened lady, dressed in a long skirt and a blouse buttoned all the way up to her sharp little chin. I'd never seen her before, which surprised me; I thought I knew almost everyone on Cranberry Island.

"I'm sorry," I said. "You startled me."

"I didn't mean to," she said in a scratchy little voice. "I like to come here from time to time, and sit."

"Me too," I said, stepping back to admire my handiwork. "What do you think?"

"They're beautiful," she said. "I love this time of year, when winter's gone and summer's on the way."

I nodded. "I thought it would never end this year."

"It was a hard one," she agreed. "I thought old Jedediah Spurrell wasn't going to make it."

"Oh?" I said politely, thinking perhaps the woman was suffering a touch of senility. She looked about eighty, and as far as I knew, there was no Jedediah on the island.

"I'm surprised we haven't met," I said, smiling. "I'm Natalie."

"I'm Lily. Born and raised here. Baptized right here in this very church." Her mouth drooped. "So was my daughter," she added quietly.

"What's your daughter's name?"

"Rose," she whispered. "I lost her when she was two. It's her birthday today."

"I'm so sorry," I said, my heart wrenching; I had never had a child, but to lose a daughter, and so young…

A cloud had passed over Lily's ancient face, but you could almost see her shaking it off. "Well," she said, clasping her withered hands. "I must be off now. Cows to milk, you know."

"Nice to meet you, Lily," I said. "I'm sorry about your daughter."

Lily smiled sadly, then rose with difficulty and hobbled toward the door. I watched her stiff back under the starched blouse, and tried to imagine her milking a cow; she looked like she belonged in a nursing home. Sometimes living on Cranberry Island was like stepping out of time.

As Lily disappeared through door, I gathered the fallen petals and headed toward the church kitchen, where Emmeline Hoyle was washing out the pans. "Got those lupines in water?" she asked, glancing at me from bright brown eyes.

"I sure did. Hey, how come I've never met Lily?"

A small furrow appeared on Emmeline's brow. "Lily?"

"She told me she and her daughter were baptized here; only her daughter Rose died when she was two." I sighed. "So sad. She said something about a Jedediah Spurrell, too."

Emmeline put down the dish she was drying. "Jedediah Spurrell died in the 1800s."

I swallowed hard. "There must be some mistake," I said. "She said she was baptized here…"

"I don't remember any Lily, either, and I've lived here all my life."

"But…"

"Natalie, I know there's been no Rose baptized here in the past fifty years. Or Lily."

"Then who was that woman?" I asked.

Emmeline dried her hands. "Show me where you saw her," Goosebumps rose on my arms as we pushed through the heavy door into the sanctuary.

"She's gone," I whispered as we crept toward the front of the church.

Everything looked the same as it had when I left. No sign of the little old woman. "I must have imagined it," I said.

Emmeline gave me an odd look, but said nothing. Together we walked around the sanctuary, then headed for the exit.

Emmeline went first, and just as I closed the heavy wooden doors behind me, something on the floor caught my eye. I stooped down and picked it up.

A petal, long and white. Nothing like the ones I'd gathered from around the altar.

"What is it?" Emmeline asked, just as a cool breeze lifted my hair, bringing with it the scent of flowers.

"Nothing," I said, cradling the lily petal in my hand. "Nothing at all."

The breeze came again, carrying the faint aroma of flowers.

Only it wasn't lupines I smelled.

It was lilies.

And unless I was mistaken, just the faintest hint of rose.

SNEAK PEEK: ANCHORED INN

Read on for a sneak peek of Anchored Inn, the tenth book of the Agatha-nominated Gray Whale Inn mysteries!

CHAPTER ONE

It's not every day an eclectic, reclusive multimillionaire rents the entire upper floor of your inn. At least not if you run a small establishment in quaint Cranberry Island, Maine.

As my niece Gwen and I went over arrangements in the cozy yellow kitchen of the Gray Whale Inn, I started fretting over all the extra requests we'd agreed to in order to host Brandon Marks. He'd made his millions (or billions) with a social media platform called WhatsIn, and despite the "social" nature of his business, he was a notorious recluse. I had no idea how he was going to manage on an island with subpar Internet, but his staff hadn't asked or added anything about it to the rather extensive list, so I hoped they'd figure it out.

"Let's go over the checklist one more time," I said

as Gwen looked over the list Brandon's assistant had sent me. Gwen had come to stay with me when I opened the inn, taking a break from her studies at UCLA to spend the summer helping out around the place while I launched the business. She'd begun painting under the auspices of the late Fernand LaChaise, and soon discovered she not only had a rare talent for watercolor, but a deep and abiding love for Cranberry Island—and for Adam Thrackton, the only Maine lobsterman I knew of to have earned a degree from Princeton.

Her mother, my sister Bridget, had been on board with the match until she figured out that Adam's work, while it did technically involve merchandise and a boat, was not in fact international shipping, but fishing. Family life had been rocky for a while, but things had finally calmed down between Bridget and Gwen, at least for the time being, and Gwen had recently started the Cranberry Island Art Guild, which provided classes for artists of all levels as well as gallery space. We'd been working together to set up some art retreats for the coming year, figuring it would boost both our businesses, and hoped to get the first promotional materials together before Christmas.

Having Gwen here at the inn was a real treat; she no longer lived above the kitchen, as she had for years, and now spent most of her days at the Art Guild, working on her own art, teaching classes, or managing the other artists. Now that it was fall, though, things were slowing down for the season, and with the sudden rush at the inn, she'd offered to help me out. My mother-in-law Catherine was pitching in, too; she'd headed to the mainland to pick up a few things Brandon's assistant had requested at the last moment and that were not readily available from the small store on the island. Gwen drew circles on the corner of the page and sighed. "I know he's gluten-free, but any other weird dietary restrictions?"

"No sugar, some dairy," I said.

"Ouch. That's a culinary challenge." She eyed the batter I was putting together. "So is it safe to assume that coffee cake you're making is not for them?"

"Correct," I said. "It's for my other guests, Max and Ellie."

"I like them," Gwen said, a faint smile crossing her face.

"So do I," I said. The two women, Max Sayers and Ellie Cox, were from Boston; Ellie owned a bookstore, and Max was her assistant manager. Evidently the trip to Cranberry Island was a post-divorce "cleansing" of sorts for Max, who had just parted ways with her husband of twenty years and was trying to figure out what to do with her life. Ellie had reserved rooms for both of them; evidently they'd become very close friends.

"I hope Max'll make it through okay; she seems nice, but shell-shocked."

"Oh, I think she will," I said. "Once she gets herself together, she'll bloom." I'd never divorced, but I'd been through a nasty break-up. It had taken a while for me to realize it, but it had been the best thing that ever happened to me. And if I hadn't gone through it, I never would have met my husband, John. I smiled just thinking about him; this morning he was down in his workshop doing a toy boat order for Island Artists. Christmas was right around the corner, so even though the inn business usually slowed down, things usually picked up in the workshop around this time of year. "Plus, she's a good egg; I can tell."

"Me too," Gwen said. "When's the bigshot coming in, by the way?"

"He's actually flying in via helicopter and then taking a private boat," I informed her. "They'll transport him directly to the dock."

She looked up at me, eyebrows practically up to her hairline. "You're joking, right?"

"Nope," I said.

"Oh, man. It's going to be like a reality show here the next few days, I'm afraid."

"You may be right," I said as I finished chopping up a few apples I'd picked from one of the many trees dotting the island. I had no idea what kind they were, but they were small, with russet and red skins, and both tart and firm, perfect for the cake I was making. "But it will help with the bank account," I reminded her as I added the apple chunks to the batter for the decadent apple-cinnamon coffee cake I was making for my non-gluten-free guests. Outside, the birch and maple trees were glowing gold and red, and the sky was a vivid blue; it was a beautiful late fall afternoon on Cranberry Island, and despite the slight worry over getting everything right for our soon-to-be-arriving finicky guest, I was feeling pretty good about life in general.

"All right, let's get through the rest of this, then. Organic detergent only on towels and sheets," my niece read, pulling her dark, curly hair up into an impromptu bun as she spoke.

"I rewashed everything and Catherine remade the bed in his room."

"Check, then. Gluten-free breakfast, coconut oil and stevia for coffee—do we have the brand of coffee he requested?"

"We do," I assured her. I'd had the special coffee

(hand-picked by free-range, organically fed baboons? Roasted over seasoned mahogany? At 40 dollars a pound, I certainly hoped so) overnighted; it had come over on the mail boat from the mainland the day before. "And Catherine's picking up the organic coconut oil on the mainland today; she's visiting a friend for dinner and will be back with it tonight."

"Good," Gwen said, looking a little green around the gills as she finished tying up her hair and made a checkmark on her list. She glanced up at me, her face a pale oval under the mass of hair; she looked drawn, I noticed, and her black cardigan sweater seemed to hang on her thin frame. "They're paying extra for all this, right?"

"A lot extra, or there's no way I'd do this." Brandon had booked the entire upper floor, taking the biggest suite for himself and the adjacent rooms for his two assistants. The other rooms were to be left vacant, lest his majesty be disturbed. It must be nice to have that kind of cash to throw around, I thought as I finished mixing the batter and poured it into the baking pan.

"Why did they pick the island, anyway?" Gwen asked.

"Evidently he likes his privacy," I told her, scraping the bowl as I spoke. "I think he's landing his helicopter just up from the dock; he paid the island a few thousand dollars for the privilege. They're going to put it toward the museum, I heard."

"So Murray Selfridge is not going to be the wealthiest guy in town for a week or two," Gwen said, grinning.

I put down the bowl and reached for the brown sugar. "Not by a long shot. I heard the Jamesons and the Karstadts are also here for the summer." Both families were long-term summer residents of the island, but didn't mingle much with the rest of us, limiting their contact to the harbormaster (they had to moor their fancy boats somewhere, after all) and the folks who took care of maintenance issues for them. It wasn't ideal, but it did provide some work and funds for islanders.

"Where did he make all his money, anyway?"

"Social media," I said as I dumped brown sugar into a small bowl and then spooned flour into the same measuring cup. I added it to the sugar with some cinnamon and butter, and set to work cutting the butter in with a fork; I could almost taste the sweet, buttery streusel already, and forced myself to remember what we were talking about instead of fantasizing about coffee cake. I looked up at Gwen. "Brandon's company went public a few years ago, and now he's wealthy enough to buy a Central American country. Maybe more than one."

"Must be nice," she said.

"I think I'd rather live on Cranberry Island," I said, truthfully. Although with the discovery of a long-missing German U-Boat a few miles off the coast a week ago, things had suddenly gotten a bit crazy. Since the team funded by Brandon had identified the wreck, just about every person on the island with a Y-chromosome had suddenly discovered a deep, hidden passion for World War II naval ships. Apparently the U-Boat in question had destroyed at least a dozen ships, some of which had borne islanders' relatives, before disappearing; Brandon was on the island in order to observe the first trip to the U-Boat with a submersible, which was expected to definitively identify the vessel.

"This whole submarine thing is a pretty big deal, isn't it?" Gwen asked as she did a last check of the list. I might not be fascinated by it, but I was happy to be hosting the funder of the expedition that had located the U-Boat, and so was half the island.

As I sprinkled the streusel over the batter, I glanced over at my niece. The drawn look worried me. "Are you okay?" I asked.

"I'm just not feeling well these past few days," she said.

"I hope it's not flu," I said.

"Me too," she said, grimacing. "At least Adam hasn't caught it. There's supposed to be bad weather coming this weekend, too; I wish he'd stay home on blustery days, but he never does."

"Good work ethic cuts both ways, doesn't it?" I said as I tucked the cake into the oven.

"It does," she said. "At least he loves his work."

As she spoke, John walked through the back door into the kitchen, smelling of paint and that particularly woodsy smell that I found so intoxicating. A cool breeze accompanied him, bringing the scent of salt air and falling leaves.

"What's in the oven?" he asked, eyeing the bowl I was about to wash. He was wearing jeans and a green plaid flannel shirt that brought out the color of his eyes. Sawdust streaked his sandy hair, and there was a fleck of red paint on his cheek, which was absolutely adorable (although I didn't tell him).

"Apple coffee cake," I informed him.

"Gluten-free?"

"No," I said. "I made some strange almond flour concoction I found online earlier today, and we'll scrambled some eggs and serve fruit salad in the morning."

"What about dinners?"

"Salmon and green beans, with sweet potato on the side and gluten-free bread from the mainland."

"Sounds like everything here is under control," he said. "I just finished painting the last batch of boats; once they dry, I'll take them to the store. I'm done in the workshop for the day, so I'm happy to take care of dinner."

"Thanks," I said, getting up on tiptoes to kiss him.

He gave me a kiss, which made me all warm inside, and accompanied it with a squeeze, then looked at Gwen. He tilted his head as he took in her wan face. "Are you okay? You don't look so hot."

"I'm just a little under the weather," she said.

I glanced at John. "She's just going over last-minute preparations. But since you're here, why don't you take that over so we can send her home to rest?"

"I'm fine," Gwen protested. "Really."

"I think we've got everything here under control," I said with more confidence than I felt. The smell of apple cake baking was beginning to permeate the kitchen; I took a deep breath of the apple-cinnamon scent, then said, "Gwen, I'm ordering you to take the rest of the afternoon off."

"Are you sure?" she asked, looking even greener than she had earlier.

"Absolutely," John told her. "Now, go home and rest."

"And take this container of chicken noodle soup with you," I said, opening the freezer and pulling out a plastic tub of soup I'd put in a few days earlier. "Do you have tea?'

"Yes, Mom," she said.

"You're welcome to curl up in your old room," I told her. "We can drive you back to the house when Adam's here."

"I... I..." She stood up suddenly, hand on her mouth, and ran up the stairs.

John and I looked at each other as she disappeared.

"I think it's best if she stayed here," I said, and put the soup back in the freezer.

"I'll leave Adam a message," John said. "And then I'll do a last check on the rooms and do the dinner prep."

"Have I mentioned recently how much I love you?"

"You have," he said with a grin, "but you know I always love to hear it again."

I was about to kiss him a second time when the phone rang.

I sighed and picked up the receiver. "Gray Whale Inn."

"Natalie? It's Charlene."

I could tell by her voice that something was very amiss with my best friend. "What's going on?" I asked, gripping the phone.

"My niece has vanished," she said.

Want to find out what happens next? Grab your copy of Anchored Inn now!

BONUS RECIPES FROM LUCY'S FARMHOUSE KITCHEN

WELCOME TO DEWBERRY FARM!

Welcome to the world of Dewberry Farm, the quaint farmhouse in Buttercup, Texas, owned by Natalie's college roommate Lucy Resnick! (You may remember meeting her in Pumpkin Pied.)

Here are three bonus recipes from Lucy's Farmhouse Kitchen, the cookbook featuring the recipes from the first six Dewberry Farm mysteries as well as several extra recipes from the farmhouse.

If you'd like to spend more time with Lucy, her poodle Chuck, escape-artist cow Blossom and the rest of the charming characters (both human and animal) in Buttercup, you can read about them in the first Dewberry Farm mystery, Killer Jam!

Enjoy!

EASY CHICKEN OR TURKEY ENCHILADAS VERDE

DEWBERRY FARM BONUS RECIPE

INGREDIENTS:

- 2 1/2 cups Verde Sauce (see recipe in sauces) or other green enchilada sauce, preferably tomatillo-based
- 1 1/4 cups crema or sour cream
- 2 cups shredded roasted chicken or turkey
- 1 4-oz. can diced Hatch green chiles (optional)
- 1-2 cups Monterrey Jack cheese
- 1 tablespoon finely chopped yellow onion
- 1/4 teaspoon kosher salt
- 1/4 cup vegetable oil
- 12 corn tortillas

DIRECTIONS:

1. Warm the tomatillo sauce in a small saucepan over low heat. Add 1 cup of the crema or sour cream and heat without letting it boil. Remove from heat and set aside.
2. In a separate saucepan over low heat, warm the chicken or turkey (add a few teaspoons of water or broth if it looks dry; you can also add the small can of Hatch green chiles at this point if you're feeling adventurous). Add the remaining 1/4 cup crema or sour cream, onion, and salt and stir to combine. Remove from heat, cover, and set aside.
3. Line a baking sheet with paper towels. Heat the oil in a small skillet over medium-high heat. When the oil is hot, add a tortilla and let it soften for a few seconds, then flip it and soften the other side and remove the tortilla to the paper-towel-lined baking sheet to drain. Repeat with the remaining tortillas.
4. Heat the oven to 350°F. Pour 1 cup of Verde sauce on a plate, put a warmed

tortilla in the sauce and immediately flip it over. Arrange 2 tablespoons of the chicken mixture in a stripe down the center of the tortilla, roll it up, and transfer to a baking dish. Continue with the remaining tortillas, adding additional sauce to the plate when necessary.

5. Pour the remaining sauce over the rolled enchiladas in the baking dish, covering the ends of the tortillas so they don't dry out in the oven. Sprinkle cheese on top, then cover the dish with foil and transfer to the oven, and bake until the enchiladas are heated through and cheese has melted, 15-20 minutes. Serve immediately.

LUCY'S APPLE DUMPLINGS

DEADLY BREW, BOOK 3

INGREDIENTS:

- Unbaked pastry for double-crust pie (use frozen from the store or your favorite recipe)
- 6 large Granny Smith apples, peeled and cored
- ½ cup butter
- ¾ cup brown sugar
- 1 teaspoon ground cinnamon
- ½ teaspoon ground nutmeg
- 3 cups water
- 2 cups white sugar
- 1 tsp vanilla extract

DIRECTIONS:

1. Preheat oven to 400 degrees and butter a 9x13 inch pan. On a lightly floured surface, roll pastry into a large rectangle, about twenty-four by sixteen inches, and cut into six square pieces. Place an apple on each pastry square with the cored opening facing upward. Cut butter into eight pieces and place one piece of butter in the opening of each apple, reserving the remaining butter for sauce. Divide the brown sugar between apples, poking some inside each cored opening and the rest around the base of each apple, and sprinkle cinnamon and nutmeg over the apples.
2. With slightly wet fingertips, bring one corner of the pastry square up to the top of the apple, then bring the opposite corner to the top and press together. Bring up the two remaining corners and seal, then slightly pinch the dough at the sides to completely seal in the apple. Repeat with the remaining apples. Place in prepared baking dish.

3. In a saucepan, combine water, white sugar, vanilla extract, and reserved butter. Place over medium heat and bring to a boil in a large saucepan. Boil for five minutes, or until sugar is dissolved, and carefully pour over dumplings.
4. Bake in preheated oven for 50 to 60 minutes. To serve, place each apple dumpling in a bowl and spoon some sauce over the top.

GRANDMA VOGEL'S LAVENDER BATH SALTS

DEWBERRY FARM BONUS RECIPE

INGREDIENTS:

- 1 cup Epsom salts
- 4 cups coarse sea salt or Kosher salt
- 1 cup baking soda
- 1 cup powdered milk (optional)
- 12 drops lavender essential oil
- 4 tablespoons lavender buds (optional)

DIRECTIONS:

1. Mix all together and store in Mason jars or Tupperware away from direct light.
2. Add 3/4-1 cup to warm bath water.

NOTE: For sore muscles, reverse the sea salt/Epsom salt ratio!

MORE BOOKS BY KAREN MACINERNEY

To download a free book and receive members-only outtakes, giveaways, short stories, recipes, and updates, join Karen's Reader's Circle at www.karenmacinerney.com! You can also join her Facebook community; she often hosts giveaways and loves getting to know her readers there.

And don't forget to follow her on BookBub to get newsflashes on new releases!

The Dewberry Farm Mysteries
Killer Jam
Fatal Frost
Deadly Brew
Mistletoe Murder
Dyeing Season
Wicked Harvest

MORE BOOKS BY KAREN MACINERNEY

Sweet Revenge, Summer/Fall 2020
Cookbook: Lucy's Farmhouse Kitchen

The Gray Whale Inn Mysteries
Murder on the Rocks
Dead and Berried
Murder Most Maine
Berried to the Hilt
Brush With Death
Death Runs Adrift
Whale of a Crime
Claws for Alarm
Scone Cold Dead
Anchored Inn
Cookbook: The Gray Whale Inn Kitchen
Blueberry Blues (A Gray Whale Inn Short Story)
Pumpkin Pied (A Gray Whale Inn Short Story)
Iced Inn (A Gray Whale Inn Short Story)
Lupine Lies (A Gray Whale Inn Short Story)

The Margie Peterson Mysteries
Mother's Day Out
Mother Knows Best
Mother's Little Helper

The Snug Harbor Mysteries
(A new cozy Maine series set at Seaside Cottage

Books in Snug Harbor, Maine! Books 1-3 coming early 2020.)

Tales of an Urban Werewolf

Howling at the Moon
On the Prowl
Leader of the Pack

ABOUT THE AUTHOR

Karen MacInerney is the USA Today bestselling author of multiple mystery series, and her victims number well into the double digits. She lives in Austin, Texas with her sassy family, Tristan, and Little Bit (a.k.a. Dog #1 and Dog #2).

Feel free to visit Karen's web site at www.karenmacinerney.com, where you can download a free book and sign up for her Readers' Circle to receive subscriber-only short stories, deleted scenes, recipes and other bonus material. You can also find her on Facebook (she spends an inordinate amount of time there), where Karen loves getting to know her readers, answering questions, and offering quirky, behind-the-scenes looks at the writing process (and life in general).

P. S. Don't forget to follow Karen on BookBub to get newsflashes on new releases!

www.karenmacinerney.com
karen@karenmacinerney.com

facebook.com/AuthorKarenMacInerney
twitter.com/KarenMacInerney

Made in United States
North Haven, CT
15 July 2022